W9-ALN-070

THE HOTEL
Westend

A MYSTERY

ASHLEY LYNCH-HARRIS

BARRINGTON
HOUSE
Publishing

The Hotel Westend (A Mystery)

Published by Barrington House Publishing
P.O. Box 47803, Tampa, FL 33646
Barrington House Publishing and its books between columns logo are registered trademarks of Barrington House Publishing.

Printed in the United States of America

Publisher's Cataloging-in-Publication

Lynch-Harris, Ashley, author.
  The Hotel Westend : a mystery / by Ashley
Lynch-Harris.
    pages cm
    Includes bibliographical references.
    LCCN 2015909989
    ISBN 978-0-9965210-0-0 (hardcover)
    ISBN 978-0-9965210-1-7 (paperback)
    ISBN 978-0-9965210-3-1 (eBook)
    ISBN 978-0-9965210-2-4 (Kindle)

    1. Women detectives--Fiction. 2. Murder--Fiction.
  3. Detective and mystery fiction. I. Title.

PS3612.Y5429H68 2015   813'.6
                 QBI15-600174

Cover designed by Humble Nations
Formatting by Benjamin Carrancho of Damonza Book Cover Design

1 Scripture taken from the NEW AMERICAN STANDARD BIBLE®, Copyright © 1960, 1962, 1963, 1968, 1971, 1972, 1973, 1975, 1977, 1995 by The Lockman Foundation. Used by permission.

2 Scripture quotations are taken from the *Holy Bible*, New Living Translation, copyright © 1996, 2004. Used by permission of Tyndale House Publishers, Inc., Carol Stream, Illinois 60188. All rights reserved.

For
My husband, Alex
My parents, Dr. Barrington and Mrs. Janel Lynch
&
In loving memory of my brother, Tremayne

Table of Contents

Chapter 1

THE GUESTS

I

SHIFTING HIS WEIGHT, Amos Hartin groaned as the less inflamed of his knees sank into the grassy plain. Peering through wide-set eyes, the hotel's elderly gardener tilted his long face downward and pressed his shovel into the soil.

"Unusual is what it is," Amos grumbled through small, pinched lips. He tugged a weed free from the soil, his bottom lip pursed in defiance. "An entire group of guests arriving and I've only just found out…"

He frowned, counting seven chrysanthemums still in their planters.

"No," he murmured decidedly. "Doesn't leave me much time at all."

The elderly man lifted his head as a commanding gust of wind swept toward him from the sea. The Hotel Westend was built on a plateau of rock that jutted out over the massive body of water; it had sheer cliffs on three of its sides. Dragging his sleeve across his brow, Amos peered at a lone seagull that squawked loudly overhead, competing with the waves' ballad strumming against the rocks below.

Amos sighed and shook his head firmly. "I'll just have to do what I can."

Drawing in a deep breath, he gave his shovel another quick, shaky thrust and plunged it deeper into the ground. This time, however, his eyebrows rose.

"Now what is *this*…?"

With a sudden burst, his spade broke through the earth and a soft thud resonated from the caked dirt that fell beside him. Gingerly he brushed his fingers over the soil and with each stroke his forehead wrinkled like a curious bloodhound.

"My goodness," he uttered, reaching for what appeared to be a dark medicine bottle. Amos glanced around but saw no one. He pinched the bottle between his fingertips and lifted it carefully above his head. The gardener turned it to and fro, watching as several pill capsules tumbled over each other.

II

The only coffee shop in Westend Bay, Gull's Café, was situated on the main street of the town, just a mile and a half from the hotel. Two women were seated outside the café, each talking on her phone without a care in the world. Inside the café was the inquisitive Mrs. Vesta Tidwell, who, in the town's opinion, often cared a bit *too* much about other people's personal affairs. Today it was the morning edition of the *Westend Gazette* that garnered Mrs. Tidwell's undivided attention.

"Well, *well*," she murmured from her corner table. "What would a *millionaire* have to do with our humble little town?"

"More pie, Mrs. Tidwell?" Lisette, the waitress, asked.

Lowering the *Gazette*, the older woman nodded.

"Have you heard, Lisette?" asked Mrs. Tidwell, brushing a stray curl from above her eye. "We've got some wealthy visitors arriving in our quaint little community—and staying at the Hotel Westend, no less."

"So I've heard, ma'am," confirmed Lisette with fashioned interest.

"I wonder what they will be like…"

Lisette smiled. "And how are your arm and your leg today, Mrs. Tidwell?"

Mrs. Tidwell looked puzzled for a moment.

"Oh!" She exhaled. "The doctor insists that I continue to wear these dreaded casts. He assures me he can remove them soon, but I can't get anywhere without help! *Complete* torture!"

Mrs. Tidwell fell some weeks ago from a rusty ladder in her back yard and broke an arm and a leg, a testament to the dangers of trimming the branches of one's apple tree. Most couldn't help but notice that, at the time of Mrs. Tidwell's disastrous incident, Mr. Humphreys and his *mistress*, Ms. Sanders, were said to have been arguing in the upstairs bedroom of the adjacent house. This, incidentally, was next to the open window…which was, of course, near to a large and now tragically asymmetrical apple tree. Needless to say, it was quite fortunate for Mrs. Tidwell that Norma Kemper, the Tidwells' longtime maid, had returned to the house in search of her watch and discovered her fallen employer instead.

"And *this*!" murmured Mrs. Tidwell to herself (for Lisette had shrewdly taken her leave). She raised the *Gazette* and frowned. "How—just *how*, in my condition, am I going to scale the steep gravel drive to the hotel?"

At the chime of the café's door, Mrs. Tidwell propped herself up with her good arm and swiftly turned her small, pointed nose toward the entryway, proving that her predatory instincts were still in good working order.

"Doris!" she called. "Doris!"

Mrs. Doris Malford, the local florist, nodded her head vigorously, her small, feathered hat sliding askew as she maneuvered excitedly between the small tables to her friend.

"Have you seen the *Gazette*?" asked Mrs. Tidwell.

"Indeed I have, Vesta," replied Mrs. Malford keenly, taking a seat. "Indeed I *have*. But have you seen the *Tribune*?"

Handing her friend the paper, she smiled broadly. Mrs. Tidwell's eyebrows rose. A mammoth-sized photo sat beneath the headline:

MILLIONAIRE RICHARD WELLING MARRIED

"My husband picked up a copy at the train station on his way back from Glassden," whispered Mrs. Malford conspiringly. "Isn't it something!"

"He has to be at *least* twice her age!" exclaimed Mrs. Tidwell. "Just *look* at her!"

Leaning forward, she smoothed the paper against the table. "Goodness, Doris!" She lifted her head. "He married an infant."

Mrs. Malford sighed. "It's like what you see in movies or read about in books, isn't it?" she considered thoughtfully, helping herself to a slice of pie. "I suppose it's like winning the lottery. Or finding a pearl in an oyster."

Mrs. Tidwell lifted the *Tribune* once more and skimmed the article. "My *goodness*," she uttered from behind the paper.

As she shook her head, strands of frazzled, wispy gray hair fell free from her bun. Mrs. Malford nodded appreciatively as Lisette placed a cup of tea on the table.

"There was no pre-nup!" declared Mrs. Tidwell, turning the page ravenously.

Mrs. Malford nodded vigorously. "Like an oyster!" she reiterated somewhat indistinctly, owing to a mouth full of pie. "Like finding an unbelievably *massive* pearl in an oyster!"

The steady rumble of a car's engine moved slowly past the café. Turning, Mrs. Malford peered through the large front windows. Her blue eyes widened.

"Vesta, that's *her*."

"What's that, Doris? Oh!" exclaimed Mrs. Tidwell, stumbling upon yet another photograph. "Just *look* at their estate!"

"Mrs. *Olivia Welling*," choked Mrs. Malford as she followed the silver Rolls-Royce with her eyes. "She's in the *car*, Vesta!"

Mrs. Tidwell looked up sharply, her mouth slightly ajar as she gazed intently ahead. A young woman in her thirties, with short black hair slicked down against her fair skin, sat comfortably in the plush luxury of hand-stitched leather seats.

"They must be headed up to the hotel now," whispered Mrs. Malford, tapping the *Gazette* decisively. "Right here, in our very own town! Imagine what a millionaire's life must be like," she remarked dreamily.

Held captive to the seat by her bulky casts, a faint whimper escaped Mrs. Tidwell as she realized that imagining was indeed all she could do.

"Isn't it something, Doris?" she remarked, reclining as the Rolls-Royce thundered away. "They can do anything they like—visit anywhere in the world, buy all the homes they want and all the clothes they like and…"

Mrs. Tidwell's voice faded. Mrs. Malford lifted her eyes curiously over the rim of her tea cup.

"Vesta?"

Drawn back into the conversation, Mrs. Tidwell remarked, "Say, that's a point, isn't it?"

Mrs. Malford replaced her cup in its saucer. "What is, dear?"

"The Wellings," said Mrs. Tidwell thoughtfully. "They *can* go anywhere in the world."

"That's right…"

Mrs. Tidwell looked at her friend.

"So why come here?"

III

Meanwhile in New York City, seated in the corner of her front sitting room, Iradene Hartwell sat upright on the plush cushion of her antique wingback chair surrounded by rich furnishings and heavy draperies. Layered in a purple brocade dress and a silver wrap that rested squarely over her shoulders, the fifty-one-year-old socialite waited impatiently for her car, resenting her upcoming trip.

"*Wretched letter!*" she uttered aloud, discreetly unfolding the ivory stationery between her fingertips. Again she read the note.

Dear Ms. Hartwell,

I hope this note finds you well. It has been quite a while, hasn't it? The last time we saw each other was at the Hotel Westend twenty years ago!

Oh! How foolish of me. You undoubtedly remember it as the McCrays' old residence, Westend Manor. My my, where has the time gone—and yet somehow it seems like only yesterday, doesn't it? Amazing how one can't remember the silliest things from just days ago while some things one never forgets. That brings me to my little idea. I thought how marvelous it would be if we had a sort of reunion. What do you think, Ms. Hartwell? We could reminisce about all that happened.

With that being said, I'd love for you to join us, as I know you certainly wouldn't want someone else to speak for you. One must be so careful of one's reputation nowadays, mustn't one? People say the strangest things...

Iradene lifted her eyes as the sound of hurried footsteps came to a stop just outside the doorway.

"Iradene," said a softly spoken voice.

She turned her face toward the door; it was a strikingly unattractive face with pale, sunken cheeks and puckered, fish-like lips.

"You're late. Where have you been?" she demanded of her far younger sister.

Marian Hartwell cast her eyes downward.

"I—I've just finished loading the car, Iradene. We are all ready to go now."

"It certainly took you long enough. Make sure that you have our travel papers in order."

Marian glanced briefly at the itinerary in her hand and silently read over the gold-embossed lettering at the top of the page: "Skylark Travel Agency". With only the subtlest lift of her chin, she confirmed, "Yes, everything is already arranged."

Without responding, Iradene's gaze darted dismissively

from her sister to the window. As she rested her small, dark eyes on her garden, she caught a glimpse of what appeared to be a man's figure disappearing beyond the garden wall.

Annoyed, she pulled back her velvet drapes and leaned forward. She scanned the grounds again but saw nothing. And yet…

Strange, thought the older woman. *I could have sworn there was somebody out there.*

IV

With only 20 minutes left until he reaches the Hotel Westend, James Rennick sat contentedly in the first-class carriage of the train, thoroughly absorbed in the *Tribune's* daily crossword. Lifting the round frames of his glasses, he rubbed absently at the bridge of his nose and quietly muttered various six-letter words.

"Hidden… H-I-D-D… No, no." He shook his head. "That won't do."

His eyes scanned from left to right, moving unhurriedly across the page.

"Maybe covert?" he mumbled. "C-O-V… No."

He straightened. A toothy grin spread across his face.

"*Secret.* S-E-C-R-E-T."

He drew his pen and filled in the empty spaces.

"Yes, that's it."

Satisfied, he laid the paper down and glanced through the window. Night was approaching as the seaside came into view; a gray hue hovered over the restless waves in the distance. A quick look at his watch revealed that it had already been forty-five minutes. *Funny*, he thought, *that I've never visited Westend Bay although I've lived such a short distance away all these years.*

James's body leaned gently against the window as the train curved swiftly around a bend. He suddenly realized he felt very tired. It had been quite some time since he had had a day off, let alone *two weeks*. Journalists didn't take time off, he had decided long ago, at least not if they wanted to move ahead. He had been just an intern then, though. Now he had his own column and he'd already had a few breaking stories. His position was secure enough to have this time away.

James drew in a deep breath, smiling as he remembered the invitation: "We at Bookworm Puzzles are happy to inform you that you've won the grand prize—an all-expense paid vacation to the Hotel Westend! Please see the attached for details. Thank you for entering."

Yes, it was good timing—that letter—and all expenses paid at that! First-class carriage, a seaside vacation, and all from my silly little hobby.

James's brows wrinkled forward.

Still can't remember entering that contest, though...

He blinked tiredly, peering once more through the window. It was night now.

Strange how darkness can mask such a massive body of water; and yet it would be foolish to think that it somehow wasn't there— that it would have just gone away.

James yawned, shifting in his seat.

"Some things will never go away," he muttered.

Closing his eyes, he drifted off to sleep.

V

Paul Hulling thumbed absently through a dog-eared copy of *Middlemarch*. Casting an anxious glance at his watch, he replaced the book on its shelf and peered toward the front doors of the New York Public Library.

Davis still hadn't arrived.

"Perhaps I shouldn't go through with this," he murmured, shrinking back behind the bookcase. "Something hasn't felt right about this whole plan from the beginni—"

Paul's cheeks reddened as he caught sight of an olive-skinned woman with dark, curly hair at the end of the aisle. She lifted her head curiously, smiling gently in his direction. Clearing his throat, he turned his attention to a set of novels, dragging his finger across their spines as he wandered discreetly toward the next bookcase.

His eyes lingered once more on the door and he flinched as his phone vibrated in his suit jacket.

"Hello?"

"Paul, it's Davis."

Paul slid further into the aisle.

"Where *are* you?" he hissed. "I was just debating whether I should forget this whole idea."

"Well, don't. And remember, *you* called me into all this."

Paul considered the man on the other end before replying.

"All right. Where would I have to go?"

"A small town by the name of Westend Bay. I hope you like water."

Paul didn't answer. Wearily he rubbed at his eyes.

"I don't see that you have any other options," said Davis. "I did my part, now you do yours."

Paul drew in a breath. "Who do I need to contact?"

"Skylark Travel Agency. A travel package has already been arranged. Your flight leaves in five hours."

Paul bit at his lip and nodded. "I better get packed."

There was a thick silence. Just as Paul was wondering whether Davis had gone, the man's voice broke in once more.

"Handle this, Paul."

Davis hesitated a moment but went on.

"Look," he started slowly, his voice gruff. "I've got a feeling it's only going to get worse. It's *already* getting worse. You *have* to handle this."

Again there was silence.

Paul glanced at his phone and confirmed that, this time, the line had indeed gone dead.

VI

Elsie Maitland cut a sharp right and pressed a bit more on the gas, her small rental car wheezing as it traversed the steep, winding road toward the Hotel Westend.

"Oh, bother—oh, bother…" she murmured, carefully maneuvering the car between the iron fencing that lined the cliff edge and the high hedges that lined the other side of the road.

Elsie winced as the engine groaned, puffing unmistakably, "I think I can, I think I can". She seriously debated whether her little locomotive really could. Pulling the wheel in the other direction, she gave a firm push on the accelerator and the car lurched forward onto level ground. Slowing her speed, the bookstore owner eased her car across the gravel drive and pulled it to a jerky stop outside the hotel.

"'Just up the hill'," she mimicked, sliding her slender legs from the car. "'*Sure* your car can make it! The old hotel is *just* up top.'" Elsie slammed the driver's door. "'Nowadays, hatchbacks are sturdier than you think!'

"Ha!"

As she retrieved her luggage, a warm mix of light and shadows washed across her smooth, brown skin.

"Just nearly sunset," she noted as a breeze swept toward her.

The green ivy climbing the hotel's stone walls fluttered gently, and the wind pulled strands of her hair from the French braid that drew snugly into a bun at the base of her neck.

Glancing at her watch, Elsie drew a deep breath and looked around. Reflexively, as was so often her habit when curious, her small, round nose bobbed up and down, gently lifting her especially thick green frames. She peered admiringly at the full-sized tennis court, which sat further off to one side of the hotel, and the chrysanthemums that lined the border of its stone walls.

"Hotel Westend," she murmured, eyeing the old wooden sign that swayed gently above the hotel's doorway.

Pulling the few wayward hairs behind her ear, Elsie collected her luggage and approached the hotel's entrance. One of two huge, antique oak doors opened, revealing the short, square build of the hotel manager. Stepping forward, his dark eyes darted watchfully behind Elsie before he finally set his owl-like face upon her. He gave a short, dry cough.

"Good afternoon, ma'am. My name is Mr. Dennis Needling. May I help you?"

"Yes, please." Elsie shifted her luggage to her side. "I'll need a room. I've gotten a bit lost. The grocer—a Mr. Reginald Glover, I believe it was—directed me here. He said you're the only hotel in town?"

Mr. Needling gave another dry cough. "That's right—" He hesitated. "Where exactly were you trying to go?"

"Oh!"

Elsie patted her pockets.

"Right. I'm afraid I'm often in the habit of losing things." She frowned and sifted through the contents of her purse. "Oh bother," she murmured, resting her hands atop her hips. "The place was a sort of bird…" She waved her painted fingernails over her head arbitrarily.

"A bird?" questioned Mr. Needling.

"Right. A pelican? A crane?"

He shook his head.

"All day you know the name of a place, but then it just suddenly slips your mind!" she exclaimed, unzipping the top compartment of her black and white-striped luggage.

Scatterbrained, thought Mr. Needling irritably.

Elsie had always been a uniquely clever woman, but one whose first impression was often marred by minor bouts of forgetfulness and disorganization. Nevertheless she carried herself with great dignity, but she was most often noticed for her selection of glasses, which had exceptionally large frames that varied in color and shape.

"Ah!"

Mr. Needling straightened, forcing a smile as Elsie unfolded a crinkled sheet of paper and quickly skimmed it over.

"Eagle's Point," she said, leveling her eyes with his.

Mr. Needling's breath caught in his throat.

"Like I said—a bird," she went on, shrugging.

Sharp eyes, he concluded silently. *Very clever, this one.*

He cleared his throat. "Eagle's Point, you say?" Squinting, he made note of the time on his watch. "No, no. That won't do; I can't arrange it in time." He sighed, peering past her.

Funny little man, thought Elsie. *Anxious like a cat.*

Mr. Needling turned his gaze abruptly on her, as though she had said the words aloud. Stepping forward, he collected her bag. "You'll need a room," he remarked. "If you'll come this way…"

Situated just beyond an old grandfather clock was the reception desk.

"That's Mr. Elbert Turnbull, our only permanent resident," whispered Mr. Needling, nodding his head toward a spacious sitting area just across from the reception desk. Facing the marble fireplace and comfortably situated in one of two wing-back chairs was a stout older gentleman, his head drooping gently to one side. The old man stirred in his chair.

"He's been a sort of long-standing guest of ours," explained Mr. Needling.

Mr. Turnbull's slack chin quivered and a faint whistle drifted upward from his lips, only to be immediately followed by two successive sniffs.

Mr. Needling continued. "The owner of our little hotel has made arrangements for Mr. Turnbull to stay here. He's become sort of a fixture of our establishment, if you will."

"If you'll just sign here, please," he instructed, collecting a key from the wall behind him. "I'm glad we could provide you accommodations," he said, nodding forward. "Please, this way."

He rushed ahead in quick, short steps across the dark, hardwood floor.

"I'm the hotel manager," he explained, looking at Elsie from the side of his eye.

"I'm Elsie Maitland."

"*Yes*," remarked Mr. Needling thoughtfully. He gave another dry cough. "I gathered that when you signed in."

Casting a furtive glance at the manager, Elsie made no reply but followed behind Mr. Needling as he ascended the oak and iron stairway. Arriving on the large landing, he turned and guided her down a long hall of doors.

"Mr. Turnbull seems quite comfortable," said Elsie.

Mr. Needling gave a breathless laugh and turned.

"Your room, Ms. Maitland," he said, pushing the door open. "You should know that the hotel actually used to be a personal residence," he explained, depositing Elsie's luggage beside the four poster bed, "but it has been years since the family…left."

Elsie listened with peaked interest as Mr. Needling continued.

"The home was soon converted into a hotel and, as a result, we have a beautiful dining hall in which we host dinner for our guests every evening at the same time: 6 pm. I'm afraid dinner has already concluded for *this* evening, but I can certainly—"

"No, that's all right," interrupted Elsie. "I'm actually a bit tired. I plan to turn in."

"Very well, Ms. Maitland. Please let me know if you need anything at all."

Mr. Needling skulked from the room and closed the door behind him.

"What a strange little man," murmured Elsie.

⁂

As night descended upon the hotel, Elsie Maitland took a seat at the cherry writing desk near to her window. Drawing the curtains, she listened to the waves as they crashed steadily against the cliffs below. She pulled a sheet of stationery from her bag and wrote:

Dear Frances,

I'm so glad I finally have a moment to write you. I love this idea you've come up with—that we should send each other letters instead of calling. Imagine if Jane Austen never left behind the letters she wrote to her sister. Imagine what little we would know about her life. It would have been a literary tragedy!

Yes, yes, I know. You have heard my stance on this, and as such I will move on to the point of this letter. As you know, I intended to travel to Eagle's Point to fulfill your fanatical request that I climb that ridiculous mountain in the shape of an eagle's head. Unfortunately—or fortunately, I'd say—I've stumbled across some other small town instead. I believe it's called Westend Bay. Apparently, the two places are hours apart, and no, I don't know how I managed it! One turn looks just like another.

Anyway, Franny, this town has got one grocer, one florist, one post office, one hotel… oh! Speaking of which, I almost died trying to drive my little rental car up the steep slope that leads to the hotel's entrance! Really, they've only got one road to get here. The other three sides are sheer cliffs leading directly into the water, with perhaps a few rocks below that you could probably walk on—if the tide were low enough, that is.

I did make note, however, of a small walking path that's got a railing beside it. I think I'll walk that route into town in the morning.

The room is nice. It overlooks the sea, but, I must admit, the hotel manager seems a bit… strange. I can't put my finger on it, but he definitely seems anxious about something—although some people are just like that, I suppose. The hotel itself is nice though. It used to be someone's home at one time. I'm sure there is plenty of history in a place like this. The architecture alone is beautiful, and the seaside is relaxing. I think I will spend a bit of time here—anything to avoid that ridiculous bird mountain!

How are things on your end? Did you find a new home healthcare worker? Hopefully she is more personable than your last. Tell Mom and Dad hello for me. Have they come back from Jamaica yet? If so, ask them if they brought me some of Grandma's coconut drops, and don't eat them this time!

I've got to get some sleep, Franny. I will write you again soon.

Love always,

—Elsie

VII

The manager of the Hotel Westend picked up the phone receiver.

"Good evening, Hotel Weste— Oh, it's you."

Mr. Needling closed the door to his office.

"Yes, I can hear you all right—it's my private line. Wait, what do you mean?"

He listened intently. It was after a few moments that he spoke again.

"Fine. I will be expecting your call. Also, we do have a few..." he paused, "...a few *unexpected* guests, but I can't imagine that they will be a problem. After all, we anticipated this as a strong possibility and nothing has to change."

Mr. Needling nodded.

"Yes, I've got it right here," he replied.

Opening the hotel guest book, he skimmed its pages.

"There is one more coming by train, but everyone else has checked in. Yes, that's right..."

Mr. Needling slid the guest book away from himself.

"No—no questions. Ok, now. Goodnight."

Hanging up the receiver, he sank slowly into his leather desk chair. Resting his hands across his chest, he thoughtfully considered the guest list.

"'Will you walk into my parlor?' said the Spider to the Fly," he mumbled quietly.

Shaking his head, he turned off the light and awaited the remaining guest.

Chapter 2
THE DINNER

"MS. MAITLAND, GOOD morning!"

Mr. Needling stretched his small lips into a smile.

"How may I be of service, today?" he asked, leaning comfortably against the reception desk.

Elsie drew a small envelope from her purse. "I just need a post office, and I would like to walk, if possible."

Mr. Needling's round head nodded eagerly. "Not a problem, Ms. Maitland. Not a problem at all. We have a post office just as you reach the bottom of the hill." He gestured in the direction of the path with his hand. "It's on the left, a few stores down. Just follow the main road. While you're there, we've also got a few delightful shops—"

"Just realized this is the evening edition!"

Mr. Needling stiffened, his eyes darting past Elsie to find a slender-built man rising from one of the chairs by the fireplace.

"Oh! Mr. Rennick," breathed the manager, his shoulders relaxing. "I didn't know anyone was sitting there."

James Rennick brushed a few dark brown curls from his forehead, only for them to fall forward once more.

"My apologies for interrupting," he replied, turning a pair of closely set eyes on Elsie. "The name's James Rennick."

Looking past her glasses, James discreetly regarded Elsie's rich, toffee-colored eyes and high cheek bones with some pleasure.

"Elsie Maitland. Nice to meet you."

"Maitland?" he asked, tilting his head to one side. "You—you're not the mystery writer, are you? I *think* that's you," he continued, this time making no secret of studying Elsie's face. "I've got one of your books, and the picture…"

Elsie smiled.

"My sister, actually—Frances," she replied. "We do resemble each other, but she is the author in our family."

James's eyes lit up. "I love her work. I do a bit of writing myself but not fiction. So it's a vacation for the two of you then?" he asked, rotating his folded newspaper above his head and appraising the hotel lobby with his eyes.

"Eh… sort of," started Elsie slowly. "Frances can't travel right now. She was injured in a jet-skiing accident almost a year ago."

"Oh, I'm sorry."

Elsie waved her hand. "Thanks, but she is recovering nicely and really she's why I'm here. I'm going on…" Elsie debated for a moment, "… I suppose you'd call them *adventures*, for the both of us."

She lifted her letter, small creases forming at the edges of her eyes as she smiled. "Writing means a great deal to Frances. So I write her about my trips and she writes back." She flushed. "A bit old-fashioned, I suppose."

"Not at all," replied James sincerely. "Actually, I like the idea."

Mr. Needling stepped out from behind his desk.

"How may I be of service, Mr. Rennick?" he asked.

"Oh, yes." James lifted his newspaper. "It's the *Tribune*," he replied. "I just realized this is yesterday's evening edition. I was wondering if you have today's?"

"Certainly, Mr. Rennick. If you'll just give me a moment."

"I've already done this one—the crosswords, I mean," he confessed to Elsie. "A sort of hobby of mine."

"You do them often?"

"I do. Won some sort of contest to stay here, in fact." James looked around the room. "I can't for the life of me even remember entering it," he laughed, shrugging, "but here I am."

"Oh dear," murmured Mr. Needling from behind the counter, searching through a stack of newspapers. "I'm sure there must be at least *one...*" He knelt down and rummaged through a cabinet beneath the front desk.

"I live in Glassden and take the train to work every day," James went on, "but the truth is my workplace isn't especially far—one stop *at most*. Really it gives me a chance to get away from everyday distractions. You'd be amazed how complete strangers will strike up a conversation with you while you're waiting at the platform."

"Forces one to stay still long enough to have a conversation," replied Elsie, smiling.

Mr. Needling dropped a pile of papers onto the counter, beads of sweat stretching across his receding hairline. "My apologies, Mr. Rennick," he interrupted. "I'm afraid we haven't received this morning's edition yet. I've searched but..."

"Oh, no worries," insisted James, folding back his copy of

yesterday's paper and sliding it across the counter. "I think I'll have a look around the town anyway before I—"

His hand stilled.

"Mr. Rennick? Is everything all right, sir?" asked the manager.

Elsie looked questioningly between James and the newspaper photo of a man and wife, recently wed.

"Yes…" James lifted his eyes. "I could have a huge story here," he muttered. "A *huge* story."

"Are you a writer?" asked Mr. Needling.

"Journalist." James skimmed the article. "They're staying *here*?" he asked.

"Yes, sir. I think you'll find we have quite an elite clientele. If you would like to consider our hotel as a possible story of interest, I'd be more than happy to tell you a bit abou—"

"But I've got to be sure," muttered James absently. "I've got to be *sure*."

He collected the newspaper and rushed from the lobby.

∽∾

Elsie quietly skimmed the pharmacy shelves, reading the labels of various hand lotions. Mr. Needling had been correct: the post office was easy to find and the quaint shops were pleasing to peruse.

At the chime of the pharmacy door, Elsie observed a tanned man with wrinkled, leathery skin rushing across the threshold; his expression was troubled. The man hesitated, considering Elsie briefly before tilting his wide brimmed hat in greeting.

"And did you decide on one, Ms. Maitland?" asked Mr. Reddy, emerging from the back room.

Mr. Reddy was a burly man of about forty-five, with trunk-like arms and a smile that reached from one side of a room to the next. Elsie could more easily picture him in a grass-stained football uniform than the spotless white lab coat he wore presently, its sleeves stretching as they struggled to contain the bulging shapes of his arms.

"I think I have," she replied, smiling. She selected a bottle with a lavender label.

"Good choice. My wife likes that one," he added.

Elsie looked around. "You know, this really is a lovely town you have here."

"We sure do like it," agreed Mr. Reddy. He rested his palms against the counter. "As I'm assuming you are staying at the Hotel Westend, be sure to have a walk by the gardens." He grinned, extending his hand to the man in the wide-brimmed hat. "Meet Amos Hartin, the gardener at your hotel."

Elsie beamed. "It was only yesterday that I was admiring your chrysanthemums," she replied as she paid Mr. Reddy for her purchase.

Amos nodded, murmuring his thanks.

Turning to leave, however, she bumped into a display case of vitamins just to the side of the register and sent the whole pile of them tumbling across the counter.

"Oh bother," she murmured, her shoulders falling.

Mr. Reddy reached for the bottles. "Allow me."

"No, please," she insisted. "I tend to make these sorts of little messes." She smiled. "It won't take me long."

Mr. Reddy nodded and turned his attention to his friend. "I had a chance to look it over for you, Amos." He retrieved a dark, plastic bottle from behind the counter and considered it with great interest. "Dug these up, you said?"

"I did," confirmed Amos. "What are they?"

Elsie shuffled a few inches closer as she peered discreetly at the gardener.

"These capsules are used to help treat insomnia," explained the pharmacist. "Basically it's a sleeping pill."

Amos leaned in.

"Is it… *lethal?*" he whispered.

The pharmacist's chest rose and fell as a deep, booming laugh escaped him. He shook his head. "Not necessarily. There is always the risk of overdose, like with any medicine, but this is a fairly common sleeping aid."

Amos grunted, scratching his chin. "Strange that it was in my flower bed though."

Mr. Reddy peered at Amos from the side of his eye.

"Don't worry, Amos," he added amicably, "these pills aren't going to kill anybody."

The pharmacy door chimed once more as Elsie exited the small shop.

"But it *is* strange," she murmured, deep in thought. "Why *would* sleeping pills be buried in his flower bed?"

❧ ☙

Paul Hulling followed Mr. Needling as he led him into the hotel's dining room. It was a beautiful dining space highlighted by two massive chandeliers, a Chippendale dining table and chairs, and a tasteful bar in the corner. It was here that Paul sought his refuge.

"A scotch," he requested, sliding onto a bar stool. He rubbed at the faint bend in the bridge of his nose. "You know what, better make it a double. I don't know how I plan to pull this off." He dragged his hands across his face.

The bartender merely nodded, as was his custom.

Standing on the other side of the room Elsie Maitland and Mr. Turnbull were engaged in a rather lively discussion.

"Now snapper—*that* is a favorite of mine," explained Mr. Turnbull, pausing only briefly to sip his wine. "I can't count the number of times I've caught handfuls—and I mean absolute *handfuls* of the fishy beasts in one trip! They just jump onto my line!

"*Sure*," he went on, arresting Elsie in her attempt to reply, "I've also caught my fair share of grouper and sea bass, but *snapper*…"

Mr. Turnbull rested his hand affectionately upon his stomach.

"Yes, that *is* something," commented Elsie.

"I haven't even told you about the things I've caught and had to throw *back*!"

"Oh, I can only imagine…"

But Elsie did not have to imagine.

"Octopus, pufferfish, scorpionfish," began Mr. Turnbull, ticking each of them off on one pudgy finger after the next. "Stingrays, jellyfish, moray eel. A baby shark!"

"I'm sure some people would have decided to keep those," considered Elsie aloud. "Many have a taste for the exotic, I expect."

Mr. Turnbull's plump face twisted in repulsion.

"Only if they are asking for trouble, my girl!"

He sniffed heartily through his nose.

"Half those fish could kill you! *Kill.* Even those approved for eating—one has to know how to prepare them. Now *I*, of course, know how, but other amateurs have nearly died trying to play around with some of those critters. A person's body temperature drops, nerves stop shooting off like they should. People think the person is dead, and they may or may not be right! What's worse, the person who's been poisoned can't tell you because they can't talk!"

"That's awful," replied Elsie.

Mr. Turnbull nodded. "I've traveled much of the world—seen it all, my girl. A real sport, fishing! And that *snapper*!"

Mr. Needling's small, owl-like face appeared in the doorway.

"Mses. Iradene and Marian Hartwell," he announced.

A pale, angry-looking woman cast a disdainful glance at the manager before walking into the dining room.

"I find that introductions help to break the ice," he murmured while retreating from the dining area.

Iradene was followed by her mousy companion, a woman in her late twenties.

"Did... did I hear that right?" stammered Mr. Turnbull. "Did he just say *Hartwell*?"

He squinted, silently cursing his failing vision.

"That's correct," confirmed Elsie, her brows rising as Mr. Turnbull retrieved his handkerchief and dabbed heavily at his forehead.

"The hotel has had very few guests as of late," remarked Mr. Turnbull thoughtfully. "They must have just arrived."

Sweeping his handkerchief across his face with some finality, he stuffed the cloth into his pocket.

"Bad news, that Ms. Hartwell," he mumbled, frowning. "And what are the odds that she would come back here?"

"*Back* here?" asked Elsie.

Mr. Turnbull didn't reply; his eyes weighed heavily on

Iradene Hartwell as she circled the dining table and finally sank into one of the Chippendale chairs.

"Get me a drink," Iradene demanded of her companion.

Elsie found the woman's voice fitting for her appearance. "Not very pleasant," she remarked, looking on.

"I'm not at all surprised, my girl. Not at all surprised."

Mr. Turnbull shifted his eyes, watching intently as the mousy brunette approached the bar, saying nothing but cautiously eyeing the man drinking a scotch.

The dining room doors opened once more.

"Mr. Richard Welling, Mrs. Olivia Welling, and Mr. James Rennick," announced Mr. Needling.

"Oh!" exclaimed Elsie, hopping to her left as Mr. Turnbull's wine glass tumbled to the floor. "Mr. Turnbull? Are you all right?"

Mr. Turnbull's face turned a crimson red.

"What is going on?" he yelled. "*What* is going on?"

He marched toward the entryway.

"Needling," he growled, his voice low and trembling. "Get me the phone."

⁓⁓

There was a moment's silence as the hotel's maid, Norma Kemper, deposited large dishes of red snapper, mashed potatoes, and green beans across the long dining table. Norma was a petite woman in her mid-twenties with dull brown hair and incredibly ordinary facial features—so ordinary, in fact, one would expect that if she entered a crowded room she would go entirely unnoticed. This, however, was not the case. Although her features were plain, her face was perpetually settled in an expression of pure bewilderment—so much so that, when first meeting Norma, people would glance over their shoulder to see what was going on behind them.

Unfortunately, with such a puzzled expression and a slightly below average aptitude for her work, society—as it tends to be—was unkind and offered Norma very little respect. Nevertheless she was determined and held her coveted post as maid for many of the residents in Westend Bay. Although serving was not her strength (the fear of fumbling fine china intimidated her), she cleaned well and offered competitive prices for her services. In fact, she had even secured arrangements to stay on at the hotel, as needed, when Mr. Needling was near full occupancy, as was the case now.

"I've got delicious potatoes," remarked Norma to Ms. Iradene Hartwell.

Iradene cast a contemptuous glance toward the young woman as she managed to deposit a small clump of potatoes on her lap.

"Oh, *ma'am*," gushed Norma. "I'm so sorry. I didn't see… It was on the side of the dish and I—I…"

"You *stupid* woman," cursed Iradene. "This dress costs more than your—"

"Heard it might rain tonight," remarked Mr. Richard Welling, his booming voice briefly distracting Iradene so that her prey could scurry out from under her paw.

"Yes," agreed Elsie, "it was a bit gusty earlier."

"Mr. Welling, isn't it?" asked Paul as he scooped a spoonful of potatoes onto his own plate. "I've seen your name in the papers. Newlywed, aren't you?"

Grinning, Mr. Welling glanced toward the slender woman seated beside him.

"Just married not more than a week ago," confirmed his wife. "Richard here insisted we come to this... quaint little town." She gave an impish smile.

"Might I just have a glass of water?" requested Marian Hartwell as Norma returned to refill their wine. "It feels a bit hot in here."

Silence gradually fell over the room as Marian nibbled shyly on her meal while Iradene remained comfortably indignant. James, on the other hand, cast curious glances around the table and, from time to time, smiled secretly into his glass. The only real distraction came from the heavy winds outside, which rattled the frames of the two large double windows that offered a view of the rear gardens.

Elsie cleared her throat.

"Mr. Turnbull would have loved this meal," she remarked. "He just spoke of his fondness for snapper. I'm surprised he has gone."

"Ha!"

Elsie became curious as Mr. Welling reclined, draping his arm across the back of his chair. "Mr. Turnbull! That cranky toad! All he does is talk about fish and sea urchins!"

"You know him then?" asked Elsie.

"I wouldn't say that I *know* him, no, but the majority of us at this table have met the man."

Iradene straightened.

"I was wondering when someone would mention it," remarked Marian quietly.

"Let's get it out then," demanded Iradene. "Why *are* we here?"

"Don't *you* know?" asked James, leaning forward. "I mean, *wouldn't* you know why you're here?"

ASHLEY LYNCH-HARRIS

"What she means", explained Mr. Welling, "is that a handful of us have actually been to this quaint little town before, twenty years ago now, and we've been invited back. Curiously enough I was given very little information as to why I should come, but since I was informed that the 'old gang' would be here I felt I ought to show up."

"So you received a letter?" asked Elsie.

"That's right, and my poor wife has had to endure," he added, gently rubbing the back of Olivia's neck. "Had to promise her the world once we've concluded our business here."

"Whatever that may be," remarked Iradene, her small lips pinched tightly together.

"You get a letter too, Ms. Hartwell?" asked Mr. Welling.

Iradene's eyes shifted from left to right, regrettably acquiring the rapt attention of the other guests.

"I did," she confirmed curtly.

Paul slowly turned his wrist, studying the wine as it stirred in his glass. "So, Mr. Welling," he clarified, lifting his eyes, "you're telling us that you, Ms. Hartwell and Mr. Turnbull were all here at this same hotel twenty years ago, and now someone has asked you back?"

"That's correct, although it wasn't a hotel back then," reflected the millionaire.

"No one seems particularly pleased by the invitation," remarked Paul.

"I'm certainly not," replied Olivia, tossing her napkin atop the table. "But Richard insisted we come."

"I wouldn't say *I'm* upset about it," added Mr. Welling. "In fact I find it… amusing."

"*Amusing*," hissed Iradene.

Marian flushed, sinking lower into her seat.

"Yes," he replied sharply. "It does make one a bit curious, doesn't it? Why go through the trouble to call the same guests together from so long ago?"

"Mr. Turnbull didn't seem very amused by it," said Elsie. "Shocked, I'd say."

"So then we've arrived at the big question," interjected James. "What exactly happened twenty years ago?"

Mr. Welling cleared his throat.

"I'll tell you what happened…"

❧ — ❧

Elsie closed the door to her bedroom and rested her back squarely against the oak frame. She considered all that she had discovered at dinner. The same feeling she had felt leaving the pharmacy washed over her once more.

"It's all so *strange*," she uttered aloud. But strange wasn't the word, she decided. No, something was *wrong*.

Taking a seat at the writing desk, Elsie began another letter.

Dear Frances,

I am surprised that I am already beginning another letter to you, as I assumed there would be very little to report in such a small town. I was, however, unpleasantly surprised to find that this is not the case. What's worse, I fear something terrible is going to happen.

Tonight I had dinner with my fellow guests of the hotel. Apparently this is not the first time these guests have come here—they were all here twenty years ago. Being that I have much to tell you, I've attached their names and what I know about each thus far. Please look them over. Once I tell you what I've discovered, you will understand why.

To the point: it is not an exaggeration to say that this was one of the most extraordinary dinners I have ever attended! First, let me begin by telling you that many of the guests were actually summoned here, and what's even more curious is that they don't know why!

It makes one wonder, then, why they would decide to come at all! Naturally, it's not difficult to presume that someone must be… twisting their arms.

That leads me to what happened twenty years ago.

Murder!

Yes, that's right. Actual murder. Mr. Richard Welling told us all about it. Do you remember that I mentioned that the Hotel Westend was originally a family home? Well, the husband, Mr. Edward McCray, and his wife, Mrs. Nancy McCray, lived here. At the time it was called Westend Manor. The McCrays had a child who was not very old—maybe about six, I was told. Anyway, Mr. McCray was business partners with Richard Welling, a guest here at the hotel. Some sort of import/export business. They were quite successful.

Ms. Iradene Hartwell, her younger sister, Marian (whom she treats like dirt and was only just a teenager at the time), and Mr. Elbert Turnbull were also present. At this point I'm not sure exactly how they were all affiliated with Mr. McCray, with the exception of Richard Welling, of course.

During their stay, the guests were awakened in the middle of the night by the sound of a child crying. They all vividly recalled running from their rooms in the direction of the noise. Naturally everyone checked the child's room, but the live-in nanny had not tucked the child in as per usual. All of the guests ran downstairs only to discover that the nanny was fast asleep, having taken some sleeping pills, and they couldn't wake her! Of course, the child was not with her. Frantic, the entire house continued their search and found that the latch on the side door leading outside (near to the nanny's quarters) had been broken by the strong wind! They rushed outside and found that the baby had managed to toddle through the side door and out toward the cliffs! The child stumbled and fell, hitting its head upon a rock and suffered an abrasion just above the right eye; but in a way this was still a fortunate accident as there were no other barriers which could have prevented it from crawling right over the cliff!

All seemed well enough (except, of course, for the professional future of the nanny) until the group, finally calm, glanced around and realized that Mr. Edward McCray was not among them—nor had he been during the entire search. The butler rushed back into the house in search of Mr. McCray, only to discover his lifeless body on the floor of his bedroom!

Dr. Charles Linder, the local doctor, was called in and declared Mr. McCray dead upon arrival: heart failure. The nanny finally came to and couldn't recall taking any sleeping pills in the first place. A cloud of suspicion settled over the house concerning Mr. McCray's death— especially on his wife, who stood to receive a sizeable life insurance payout. Of course, one would expect a proper investigation to have taken place, as the whole incident seemed sketchy (and was quite the talk of the town, no doubt), but the Chief of Police determined the case closed! Mr. McCray did have a history of heart problems and the nanny could have simply forgotten she had taken the sleeping pills.

As far as the wife's motive, the investigator explained that the insurance money couldn't have been a real motive because they later found out that the wife never collected it! Odd, don't you think? There was a quick burial and the wife and child left Westend Bay immediately after.

Small towns, however, live for scandal and they weren't going to just let this bit of juicy news go to rest! The residents demanded that the Chief of Police reopen the case, but he didn't budge—said he could care less what they wanted. The McCray estate was soon bought out and made into a hotel, and at the end of his term the Chief of Police retired and moved on—literally moved away. Rumor has it that he is living quite comfortably a few towns over.

The town wasn't pleased, of course, but the outcry of injustice fell silent when residents realized that the hotel brought tourists… which brought money to their humble seaside town, boosting profits for their small businesses.

Now twenty years have passed and the same people previously involved in that case have been gathered together by person or persons unknown. It seems like some sort of sick game is going to begin, Franny. The pieces have been positioned and now it's just a matter of waiting on the first move…

❧ ❦

The hotel fell quiet as everyone had dispersed to their rooms with the exception of Mr. Turnbull who had settled into his usual chair in the lobby.

I've done all I can do. Yes, all I can do…

With eyelids drooping, he reclined further into his chair. He was in a pensive mood.

That was a shocking evening, he thought to himself. *A shocking evening, indeed!* He turned his head. No one was around. *Probably all in bed*, he decided. *Perhaps I ought to go to* my *bed.* Mighty gusts of wind blew outside the hotel as the fire crackled soothingly before him. *No, I'll stay down here a little while longer.*

Mr. Turnbull reflected on Mr. Welling and his new, young wife.

"Ha! Old fool!" he exclaimed aloud.

He then thought of Ms. Maitland. *Nice young woman. Likes to fish.* He suddenly felt hungry. *I missed a good meal of snapper tonight.*

He shifted to a more comfortable position, his head slowly falling back against the headrest. In protest, he forced it up once more and peered ahead through tired eyes.

And then there's that young man! Just traipsing into the dining room. He shook his head. *No, I still can't believe he's here.*

Mr. Turnbull lifted his eyes and grunted as Walton, the hotel's chef, passed by with a nod.

Now, he's *quite young too—but a good cook. Reliable fellow,* thought Mr. Turnbull approvingly.

His head tilted once more, but this time it fell to the left. He was beginning to give way to the fatigue.

"The Hartwells," he murmured.

Iradene has always been a nasty bit of work, but that Marian... now, she seems a bit strange—a quiet one. A bit clammy too. Never did understand the younger generation's aversion to vitamins.

He rubbed his fingers thoughtfully across his chin, brushing against the coarse stubble.

And what about the way she looked when she saw that man at the bar? Went a bit pale. Very strange indeed. What was it? Shock? Maybe... But perhaps it was fear? Yes, seemed a lot like fear.

At this thought, Mr. Turnbull allowed his heavy eyelids to rest.

Chapter 3
REVEREND PENNINGTON

THE TIPS OF Elsie Maitland's fingers crept clumsily across the top of her night stand. Grasping for her glasses, she stumbled out of bed and felt her way through the dark room toward the bathroom. As she passed her bedroom door, however, two soft clicking sounds echoed from somewhere down the hall—then footsteps. Yes, she definitely heard footsteps.

Elsie lingered, pressing her ear to the door. She bit anxiously at the inside of her lip as she listened intently to a woman speaking.

"What are you doing here?" the woman asked.

Elsie held her breath as a man's voice answered.

"Isn't that obvious?" he asked, his voice barely above a whisper.

The man paused for a moment before starting again.

"I—I thought you would have *wanted* me here," he said, but the woman made no reply.

There was silence for a moment until finally the man spoke once more.

"I've found something out," he murmured. "I've got something I need to show you."

The woman groaned.

"No, don't go," he pleaded.

Elsie frowned as the sound of their footsteps shuffled across the carpeted hall.

"Let go of my arm," demanded the woman.

"I'm sorry. I didn't mean…" The man cleared his throat. "It's just that you *really* do need to listen to what I have to tell you."

"Why is it all so complicated?" the woman murmured, the pitch of her voice rising.

"But it *isn't* complicated. You know what has to be done."

"It's not that simple", the woman whispered sharply in reply, "and you know that already."

The man snorted. "But it is. *You're* just not willing to go through with it. But don't you see? It *has* to be you. I can't do it for you."

Elsie pressed her ear closer to the door as neither said anything for a moment.

"I see. Well, cheers to death then," he added suddenly, his speech running together.

"*Death?*" echoed the woman.

The man's voice was slow and steady in reply.

"It seems to me that the only way our little problem will be solved is if she dies."

Footsteps rushed away from Elsie's room and the sound of a door softly closing could be heard further down the hallway.

⚮

"Thirty–Love!" yelled Olivia Welling, striking the tennis ball over the net.

Paul Hulling sprang forward and answered the serve with a solid backhand. Olivia darted left in response. Dipping low, she thrashed at the ball and it tore past Paul mercilessly.

"That's in!" she yelled.

"My wife thinks it's Wimbledon!" shouted Mr. Welling, raising his beer in good humor.

Under the shade of the hotel's gazebo that was situated just off to the side of the tennis courts Elsie smiled at Mr. Welling from across the table as James approached from the hotel. He took a seat beside her, seeking shelter from the noon sun.

"Your wife has got a good hand," complimented James, reclining in his chair.

"She loves the game," agreed Mr. Welling. "Used to play before I met her—in Dansford. Small town. Small tournaments." Mr. Welling shrugged and took a slow, appreciative sip of his drink. "She has a tennis coach for a mother," he went on. "Ruthless woman, I hear, from what Olivia's told me, but I've only met her a few times."

"Expects perfection on the court?" asked Elsie, pouring a handful of cashews into her palm.

"There and everywhere else," confirmed Mr. Welling. "Her mother raised her alone, though." He was thoughtful for a moment. "You really can't fault the woman for trying to prepare her daughter for life, can you?"

"No, I suppose not," replied Elsie, fighting back a yawn. She stared into her glass and absently stirred her daiquiri.

"You seem a bit tired, Ms. Maitland," remarked James.

"A bit," she admitted. "Had trouble sleeping last night…"

"Do you play tennis?" he asked.

Elsie fell back into her chair, shaking her head. "I've never been much for tennis. The concept that the ball ought to go *over* the net always seems to elude my natural skill set. Better for everyone, I think, that I don't play." She took a sip of her daiquiri.

"That bad, huh?" James replied, stifling his laugh. "Well, I never could master the backhand."

Olivia, dressed in a white tennis skirt and blue tank, collapsed into her chair beside her husband.

"Good game, Mr. Hulling!" she said, resting her racket on the table.

"For you, I think," replied Paul amicably, also taking a seat. "Your wife's got a vicious streak in her, Mr. Welling!"

"One of the qualities I like in her!"

Olivia pressed a cold bottle of water against her forehead.

"Our stay has been nice enough, Richard," she grumbled, "but *when* will your business here be done? Tennis is all this pitiful little town has to offer!"

"You're not leaving already?" asked James.

"I hope so," Olivia replied.

"I've actually decided to leave as well," added Elsie. "With everything that has been discussed, I can't say that I'm too eager to stay either."

"Really?" said Paul. "I'm the opposite. I'm curious about this twenty-year-old murder and *why* you've really been called here." Paul directed his gaze at Mr. Welling.

"Me too," agreed James, drawing his chair closer. "What is the point of it all?"

"I couldn't tell you," replied Mr. Welling in earnest. "I

found it amusing at first, but now I see that coming out here has just been a waste of time."

"Mr. Welling," Elsie remarked, "may I ask, what did your letter say to convince you to come here in the first place?"

Mr. Welling grinned and took a sip of his beer.

"The letter stated that I should come and defend my reputation, if you will. Vague letter—wasn't even signed—but the gist of it was that if I didn't come someone might say something untrue about what happened twenty years ago. I've got a lot of big clients, you understand? Can't risk slander, not with murder cases. In the business world people aren't very forgiving if your name is tied up with murder, no matter what actually happened."

Mr. Welling finished his drink.

"But I now see", he added decidedly, "that this has just been a waste of time—some kind of stupid joke. No one has even contacted me since we arrived."

He looked toward his wife.

"You only have one honeymoon in life and you should be enjoying it. We'll leave first thing in the morning. I'll have our travel agent make us new arrangements. Pick anywhere you like, Olivia."

❧ ❧

"Ms. Maitland!"

Elsie crossed through the hotel's front doors to find Mr. Needling scurrying out from behind the front desk.

"A letter has arrived for you—priority mail."

"Thank you, Mr. Needling."

Unsealing the envelope, Elsie took a seat in one of the

chairs by the fireplace. *The ambiance*, thought Elsie with some amusement, *is quite different without Mr. Turnbull dozing in the chair beside me.* She reclined, smiling as she recognized her sister's handwriting.

"Dear El. My, what an interesting place you've stumbled upon! How thrilling!!"

Elsie's eyes grew wide. She wasn't so sure she agreed with Frances, but she read on.

You have to find out more, El! There has to be a reason the same guests have been gathered together. You've got a real life mystery on your hands! Let's solve it!

"This is just like Frances," muttered Elsie.

My first question is: where are the wife and child now? They have essentially vanished since that incident so many years ago. Today, the wife would be an older woman and the child would be in his or her mid-twenties… maybe thirty years of age at the most? Of course, they could still go by their own names, but what would be the point? Leaving their home behind the way they did suggests that they wanted to be as far away from what happened as possible. So my theory is that they have new names, new identities. Yes, that's how I'd write it in one of my books. Remember one of my first mysteries: No Longer Abram? *The main character left everything he knew behind and started again.*

My next question—and this is critical—is: who would <u>want</u> to rake up such an old murder? What possible motive could there be? Who would benefit?

Oh, El! You'll have to keep me updated! I will reply immediately, I promise. Just keep me in the loop. This is far too exciting to ignore. And I know you, El. You've probably already packed your bags, but unpack! I need you to gather as much information as humanly possible so that we can determine what's going on. This is just what I need to keep me from going stir-crazy!

Speaking of which, I've got a new physical therapist now. Mom, Dad and I hired her on a sort of trial basis. We hope therapy from home will alleviate some of the stress from all these changes. Her name is Bernadine. She has a squeaky voice and is lovably round and sort of squishy around the edges, if you know what I mean. No, of course you don't! It makes no sense unless you meet her, but I can tell you that I liked her right off the bat. She really is a funny sort of person but without trying to be. There is nothing clear or concise about the manner in which she communicates. You've got to sort of drag it out of her at times, but we get along well. She's really very clever but you wouldn't tell just by looking at her—you've got to figure out how she thinks first. Like I said: squishy.

Finally, to answer your question, yes, I'm well, little sister. No worries on this end. Grandma did make you some coconut drops and I only had a small taste…

And then there were eight… (Bwahahaha!)

Mom and Dad told me to tell you hi and let you know that Lawrence is running your bookstore like a pro! Only one small fire, but it was confined to just a single shelf. No harm done! Hehe.

Love you lots, El. Remember, keep me posted! We've got a mystery to solve.

—Franny

Elsie grinned and shook her head as a silver-haired man in a black shirt and white collar settled into the chair beside her.

"Pardon me if I've interrupted you," he said, glancing at Elsie's letter through square frames. "I'm waiting for a room."

"Not at all. I've just finished..." Elsie debated, "...is it 'Reverend'?"

The man extended his hand.

"Yes, Reverend Pennington."

"Elsie Maitland," she replied. "It's a pleasure to meet you."

The reverend slid his small carry-on beside the chair.

"So *hot*, isn't it?" he commented, retrieving a handkerchief from his pocket.

"It is. I've just come in from outside myself."

"Ah! But you'll cool off in no time." The reverend tugged gently on his collar. "My internal AC unit has been on the fritz for years! I keep my home at a steady 73 degrees. Thank God for salvation, is all I can say!" he exclaimed, dabbing repeatedly at his forehead. "I couldn't take eternity in hell, Ms. Maitland. Far too hot!"

Elsie bit back her smile.

"You may laugh, but I had a hearty sermon on *that*, I can tell you! One of my more loquacious moments."

"No, I agree," replied Elsie truthfully.

The reverend straightened, pocketing his handkerchief.

"Been here long?" he asked, taking a breath.

"Just a couple days. Really I was planning on leaving soon, but I'm not so sure anymore. I think I might stay another day."

Elsie glanced thoughtfully at her sister's letter as Frances' words ran through her mind.

"Not on pressing business then?" asked the reverend.

"To be honest," replied Elsie, "I'm not sure."

He offered a friendly smile and remarked, "It was just yesterday that I was asked to come here, but now I'm wondering if I should have called first." He looked with concern toward the front desk, his large, pointed nose an outstanding feature of his profile, in every manner of speaking. "They don't quite have a room ready."

"You received... a letter, perhaps?" probed Elsie cautiously.

The reverend turned his head, surprised.

"A letter? No. Not at all." His forehead creased. "Just a phone call," he replied, dabbing the perspiration from his head once more.

Elsie flushed. Lifting her own letter, she remarked, "Perhaps I am one of the only few who write nowadays."

"Oh! Not true, my dear! I write letters quite a bit. So personal, don't you think?"

The reverend tugged repeatedly at his shirt, gently fanning himself with the polyester fabric.

"I'll need a mop in a minute," he mumbled, inspecting the space around his chair. "They'll have to set out safety cones. Yes, bright yellow signs all around me with little stick-figure men slipping on puddles, arms flailing and legs bent in awkward positions." The reverend's bottom lip puckered.

Elsie held back her laughter and cleared her throat. Hastily, she returned to their previous topic.

"Yes... So, someone called you to come?" she asked.

The reverend lifted his head, puzzled.

"I'm sorry?"

"To come to the hotel," clarified Elsie. "You said that someone called you?"

"Of course, yes! On a matter that seemed quite urgent." He scooted forward in his chair. "It appears that someone needs

my help and asked me to come to this hotel. Of course, I'm
not especially far from here—in Dansford—and I thought, if
I'm needed, I *ought* to come, shouldn't I? So as you can clearly
see I—"

A bell chimed. This time both Reverend Pennington and
Elsie turned their eyes toward the front desk.

"Well, if that isn't Ms. Iradene Hartwell," mused the
reverend.

Iradene and Marian Hartwell waited as Mr. Needling
sorted through the mail.

"You know the Hartwells?" asked Elsie, surprised.

"From quite some time ago," confirmed the reverend. He
suddenly recognized the pale brunette standing beside Iradene.
"That must be *Marian* Hartwell. She was so young, just a baby
when I met her! Must be in her early thirties now."

He looked at Elsie.

"I married their parents, you know? Was quite close to
their father for a time, but my ministry moved me all over the
United States. Still, I eventually met the children much later."

The reverend sighed.

"The Hartwells have had such tragedy. Iradene was the
only child for some time. Their parents had her in their first
year of marriage. In fact, she was already at least eighteen years
old when Marian came along—a pleasant surprise, of course.
I don't think they expected to have any more children. Their
mother, however, experienced complications. Marian was born
a healthy baby, but their mother did not make it through
the pregnancy. Mr. Hartwell—their father—tragically passed
some years later in a car accident, leaving Iradene responsible
for them both."

"That must have been incredibly difficult," said Elsie.

"I can only imagine," he agreed. "Fortunately Mr. Hartwell had the gumption to make all the legal arrangements for his daughters—financially, I mean. So in that regard, at least, they never had to struggle."

The reverend looked toward the front desk to find that the Hartwells had departed.

"I hope my coming here does prove helpful," he murmured softly.

Elsie studied him. "Who exactly needs your help, Reverend?"

"Can't say," he replied. "The thing is, I know *who* called me, but I don't know exactly *how* I can be of help. You must think I'm strange!"

"You would think", murmured Elsie, "but no, actually. Not here, at least."

Reverend Pennington reclined. "I suppose there's no harm in telling you that I was asked to come for the sake of… righteousness. For the sake of uncovering the truth."

"Pardon?"

"Apparently", he explained, "I can somehow help in setting things right in some way. So I was told, at least!"

Elsie wondered aloud, "And that was enough for you to pack a bag and come *here*?"

The reverend laughed.

"May I tell you a story, Ms. Maitland?"

"Please do."

He leaned forward and settled his arms on his knees.

"Many years ago", he began, "a few of my colleagues and I had the opportunity to study under the tutelage of a vicar in a small village much like this one—a village in England. It was early in our ministry and a very exciting time for us. Perhaps too exciting, as soon after we arrived a man was found murdered in the vicar's study! Needless to say an investigation took place, but the police seemed to be making little progress. There was, however, a woman—a seemingly ordinary, elderly woman—the very kind who knits, gardens and carries large floral handbags filled with yarn and ribbon, or whatever it is elderly women carry."

Elsie peered questioningly at the reverend.

"What I mean", he continued, "is that it was *she* who solved the murder—a very, *very* clever murder." He considered for a moment, smiling. "A very clever *woman*."

The reverend shifted forward in his seat.

"I asked her once," he reflected aloud, "when the congregation had gone and she had stayed behind to replace a vase of wilted flowers, what she thought of justice."

"Justice?" asked Elsie.

"Just so," he nodded and smiled. "Her reply was simple: 'Let justice roll down like waters. And righteousness like an ever-flowing stream'."

Elsie smiled. "She sounds like an extraordinary woman."

"I do believe she was," agreed the reverend. "She didn't readily trust people, but she still accepted them kindly."

"I think I would have liked her very much," said Elsie.

"I think so too," he agreed. "And that's just it, Ms. Maitland. *I* want to see 'a mighty flood of justice, an endless river of righteous living'; but I not only hope, I *do*, you understand?"

"I think so…"

"In this fallen world, Ms. Maitland, I am called to take *action*, and someone here needs my help. Therefore, I will try to help however I can."

The reverend beamed.

"So here I am, to help set things right in some way, even

if I'm not sure just how yet." He chuckled, his smile softening as he reflected. "*Wait...* that's not true," he started slowly, his tone curious. "Now that I think about it, I was told how I can help."

The reverend fixed his eyes on Elsie.

"Apparently, I can uncover the truth."

<hr>

It was well past midnight and all the other guests had gone to sleep hours ago, but Paul and James had found that they had much in common. Commandeering Mr. Turnbull's sitting area, the two had conversed quite easily through the later part of the night and well into the early morning hours. The moon cast shadows in the dimly lit hall as the two men walked quietly toward their rooms.

"She's not a nice woman, Ms. Iradene Hartwell," said Paul Hulling with a small glass in his hand.

"So I've heard," replied James dryly.

Paul took a long sip of his drink.

"What makes you dislike her so much?" asked James quietly.

"Not just me," corrected Paul with a sternly pointed finger. "That woman has got a dark past. Blackmail, fraud—she's a manipulative type of woman. Just look at how she treats her own sister, flesh and blood."

"I see," he replied. After a pause, James continued: "Yes, Ms. Iradene does seem a bit difficult, but there are a lot of relationships—sibling or otherwise—that are a bit... off."

Distracted, Paul stopped. "You heard that?"

James listened.

"No…" he started slowly, "I didn't hea—" He listened more closely. Turning, he returned silently in the direction of the stairs. "I *did*, as a matter of fact," he whispered.

"There it is again," said Paul sharply.

"Is it…" James faced Paul. "Is it a *baby* crying?"

The door to Iradene Hartwell's room swung open and she emerged.

"What is that noise?!" she demanded. "I can't sleep like this. Where is Mr. Needling?"

"Then you can hear it too?" asked Paul.

"*Of course* I can hear it. Why else would I be out here?"

"Has someone got a *baby*?" called another, deeper voice from several doors down. Mr. Elbert Turnbull lumbered from his room, a robe tied precariously about his round waist.

"I swear the crying is getting louder," said James. "The child may be hurt."

"Someone wake Mr. Needling," instructed Paul.

Mr. Turnbull responded and went to knock upon the manager's door at the end of the hall.

Elsie stepped from her own room.

"He's not in there," called Mr. Turnbull.

"I hear a baby…" started Elsie.

"There is a baby *somewhere*," called James. "We've got to start looking."

"Where is it coming from?" asked Paul. "Downstairs?"

"I think so," said Mr. Turnbull, his voice drowsy. Clearing his throat, he added, "I heard it just outside, as though it was outside my window? I can't be sure…"

Paul knocked hurriedly on the other doors. "Get up! We need your help!"

Reverend Pennington peered into the hall.

"*Outside?*" said Elsie, jolted awake by Mr. Turnbull's suggestion. "*The cliffs!*"

Richard and Olivia Welling emerged from their room.

"Miss Olivia?" said the reverend, squinting curiously from the threshold of his room.

Olivia Welling slunk back behind her door.

"Help us find the baby!" yelled James.

"A *baby*?!" questioned Mr. Welling, dutifully following behind James and Elsie as they set off toward the stairs.

"My robe!" yelled Olivia to her husband. "Go on without me, I'll be right behind."

The reverend tilted back his head, his nose scrunching upward as he tried to identify the blurry figures rushing down the hall.

"My glasses," he murmured, turning back into his room. "Can't see like I used to."

"The front door is locked!" yelled Paul as James arrived at the foot of the stairs.

James turned down the hall toward the kitchen. In the distance was the servant's door, open and leading out to the cliffs. James was rushing down the hall, calling for the others, when another voice shouted from one of the downstairs rooms.

"I can't wake Norma! I can't wake her!"

Elsie's steps faltered.

"Mr. Needling?" she said, peering into the small room. "What happened to…"

"I can't wake Norma!" he yelled over his shoulder, shaking the maid's arm.

"Do you see the baby?!" called James.

Elsie ran on, stepping out into the cold night. She wrapped her robe more snugly around her waist.

"Does *anyone* see a baby?!" called Paul.

A curse came from Mr. Welling several feet away.

"Have you found something?" called James.

"I found something all right," yelled Mr. Welling. "I found our 'crying baby'."

In his hand was a voice recorder, the sound of a baby still wailing through its speakers.

"What kind of a sick joke is all this?!" he yelled, throwing the recorder to the ground.

Olivia met her husband and slid her arm into his.

Elsie peered searchingly around her.

"Has anyone seen the reverend?" she asked. "Reverend Pennington…"

"Pennington?" asked Paul.

"Yes, an elderly man. He is staying at the hotel. I thought I saw him come from his room…"

"Why we've been dragged out here in the middle of the night, I have no idea," interjected Iradene, her face twisted in disgust, "but this ridiculous fiasco is unacceptable! I'm returning to bed."

"I'll go and check on the reverend," said James quietly to Elsie.

Inside, Mr. Needling fumbled with the phone, replacing the receiver after leaving an urgent message for Dr. Linder.

"What's the meaning of all this, Needling?!" yelled Mr. Welling, his broad frame moving quickly past the manager.

Mr. Needling scurried behind. "I—I'm so sorry, but I don't know what you mean?"

"Sick joke! That's what this whole business is!"

James called from the top of the stairs. "Come quickly! It's the reverend!"

At the foot of his bed, Reverend Pennington lay face down on the floor, the bloodied base of a lamp beside him. Silence briefly stretched across the stunned faces congregated at the reverend's door. James ventured a step toward the body and reached two shaky fingers toward the man's neck.

"Is… is he…?" stuttered Olivia, her face pale.

James nodded. "I'm afraid so."

"Who would want to kill the reverend?" cried Elsie, her voice unsteady.

"Move out the way! *Move* out the way!"

A man of about sixty-five and of average build pushed through the doorway and stumbled over to the lifeless body of Reverend Pennington.

"Dr. Linder!" exclaimed Mr. Needling, his small lips parted in surprise. "How—how did you get here so quickly?! I only just tried to reach you…"

"I was already here on behalf of another patient. Now, if you could all please back away from the body."

"It's just like last time," growled Mr. Turnbull. "A child crying! The maid's been drugged—knocked out, asleep! A man is *dead* and now the *exact* same doctor from twenty years ago is hunched over the body!"

"No, Mr. Turnbull. It's not all the same!" yelled Paul, reaching the top of the stairs.

Mr. Turnbull turned. Crossing the threshold, Paul leaned forward, his hands pressed against his knees.

"It's not the same," he echoed between breaths. "This time, sir, we can't wake the maid."

Dr. Linder stood. "Then I must see her."

"Sir," said Paul, straightening. "She's dead."

Chapter 4
SERGEANT WILCOX INVESTIGATES

AS THE MORNING sun settled on Westend Bay one topic of discussion seemed especially prominent among the residents. At 80 North Shady Glen Road, Mrs. Vesta Tidwell sat across from her husband at the breakfast table as they read the morning *Gazette*.

"Oh! How *terrible*. I can't believe it," she muttered in bewilderment.

Mr. Tidwell sniffed indignantly. "How can a man expect to save for retirement when the dollar keeps deteriorating as it does?"

"Yes, George, but listen to this."

"It's absolute nonsense!"

He turned the page.

"You *must* listen, George."

Mr. Tidwell seemed to show little interest in anything other than his fish market, small garden, and the inevitable decline of his retirement fund. As such, for Mr. Tidwell to take notice of a news story of any kind was a testament to its sensationalism.

"Yes, dear," replied Mr. Tidwell indulgently from behind the *Gazette's* financial pages. "I'm listening."

"There have been *two* murders!" exclaimed Mrs. Tidwell. "Here in *Westend*!"

At that moment not only did Mr. Tidwell's bushy brows rise, his paper also descended.

Mrs. Tidwell drew in a startled breath and stammered on.

"*Our* very own maid, George, was *poisoned*, and another guest at the hotel—some reverend—was bludgeoned on the head! Imagine! *Murdering* a man of the cloth!"

"This is unbelievable," replied Mr. Tidwell. "Does the paper say who did it?"

Mrs. Tidwell's face had fallen.

"No, no it doesn't." She hesitated and then remarked, "That's why I need you to go and find out for me."

Mr. Tidwell's brows darted upward once more, this time in disapproval.

"I'm *bound*, George!" Mrs. Tidwell lifted her arm in its cast. "And I'll just die if I can't find out more!" She leaned forward. "Can't you just deliver some fish to Mr. Needling? Find out what's gone on?"

"I'm not due to make another delivery, Vesta. Not for another day or so. Besides, we have no reason to intervene in this business. Let Sergeant Wilcox sort it out."

He lifted his paper.

Mr. George Tidwell was usually a thoroughly patient man, particularly in showing feigned interest in his wife's gossiping. In fact, the women of Westend Bay were of the opinion that Mr. Tidwell must be a good-natured man to tolerate such a busybody wife. The men of Westend's Empire Club, however, questioned the accuracy of this explanation and sought to find their own.

"It can't be her looks," they debated, exchanging puffs of their cigars.

"Well surely she must offer something."

"Kids?"

"No, no kids."

"I hear she's got a pretty bit of money coming her way once that distant uncle of hers passes on."

"Ah!"

Still, none of these arguments were ever confirmed either way since Mr. Tidwell seemed to show little interest in the opinions of others and to Mrs. Tidwell's dismay this was now the case as he remained buried in the paper. However, the details surrounding the murder dominated Mrs. Tidwell's mind.

"Oh! George, you're intolerable!" Mrs. Tidwell screwed up her nose. "I won't stop until you go! *George…*"

⁂

Meanwhile, back at the hotel, Sergeant Wilcox, looking a lot like a bulldog with a heavy, thick-set frame, and a distinctively pushed-in nose, sat stiffly across from Mr. Needling.

"We appreciate the use of your office, Mr. Needling," remarked the sergeant.

Mr. Needling gave a short, dry cough. "Of course. Anything to help."

A knock came at the door.

"Yes?" called the sergeant.

Elsie poked her head into the room, her large, sky-blue, rectangular glasses sliding toward the tip of her nose.

"Excuse me, Sergeant," she remarked, tugging gently on the sleeves of her blouse. "I was wondering if it would be all right that I go into town, just to visit a few of the shops."

The sergeant grunted.

"That will be fine," he replied. "Just remember that this is a murder inquiry, Ms. Maitland. I will be expecting all of you to remain close should there be further questions."

The door widened and Mr. Tidwell, holding a basket of fish, peered into the room.

"I'm sorry to interrupt," he said, his eyes wandering between the sergeant and Mr. Needling. He looked curiously toward Elsie and then returned his attention to the hotel manager.

"I've got your weekly delivery, Dennis," he said, lifting his basket.

"A bit early, isn't it?" asked the manager.

Mr. Tidwell blushed.

"The wife sent me," he confessed. "For my sanity, you understand? I had no choice but to concede."

Both the sergeant and Mr. Needling had met Mrs. Tidwell. They nodded.

"That will have to wait, Mr. Tidwell," replied the sergeant, signaling him toward the door with an abrupt motion of his head. "Ms. Maitland, have you already provided your statement to my officer?"

"I have."

"Then I will speak with you when you return."

Elsie nodded, but lingered in the hall just out of Sergeant Wilcox's view.

"And as for you, Mr. Tidwell," he continued, "tell your wife that there have been no new developments. We're not running a gossip station here."

"Of course, sir."

Sergeant Wilcox turned his back. "Now, Mr. Needling, were you at the hotel the entire night?"

"Yes, sir, I was."

Mr. Tidwell slowly closed the door behind him.

"I'm George Tidwell," he whispered to Elsie as they walked toward the lobby, his eyes crinkling at the corners as he smiled. "I own the local fish market here in town."

"Nice to meet you, Mr. Tidwell. I'm Elsie Maitland, just a guest here."

Mr. Tidwell raised his voice as the two stepped into the hotel's lobby.

"So, you were here when the murders…" he hesitated.

"I was," confirmed Elsie. "Although I can't say that I know much about what happened. It's all so terrible and strange…"

Mr. Tidwell contemplated for a moment.

"Strange? How do you mean?" he asked, resting his basket on top of the reception desk.

Elsie's cheeks warmed. "It's just… it seems this has all happened before—twenty years ago, I've heard."

"Yes," Mr. Tidwell reflected, "there was a murder back then."

"No," pressed Elsie, "I mean this happened *exactly* as before. There were a lot of similarities in today's case to the one twenty years ago."

"Oh… *oh*," comprehended Mr. Tidwell. "Does this tie in, then…" he lowered his voice, "…does this tie in with the McCray murder?"

"I can't say," stated Elsie. "I guess I'm just a bit perplexed by it all."

Mr. Tidwell nodded, lifting his basket from the desk.

"I see why you'd find this unsettling," he replied. Then, smiling gently, he added, "Our sergeant is very good at what he does, Ms. Maitland. He will get to the bottom of this."

Turning toward the kitchen, he remarked, "Now if you'll excuse me, I should put this fish on ice. I expect that Mr. Needling will be a while, but Walton can take it."

"Of course," replied Elsie, her thoughts elsewhere as Mr. Tidwell walked away. "The McCray murder…" she murmured.

She lifted her eyes to find Mr. Tidwell disappearing through the kitchen door.

"Mr. Tidwell!" she called, hurrying toward him.

He turned, surprised. "Yes, Ms. Maitland?"

"Did you know Mr. McCray?" she asked.

Mr. Tidwell's eyes fell.

"I did. Knew him better than most, I'd say. Elbert Turnbull, Edward McCray and I would take the boat out at least a couple times a month to go deep-sea fishing." He grinned. "They sure could catch their own fish, but they were still some of my best customers." He reflected. "Edward McCray was a good man. Sad he's gone."

"Mr. Turnbull's still here, at the hotel, you know?" remarked Elsie.

Mr. Tidwell smiled. "I sure do. We don't do much fishing anymore, but I still see Elbert every week when I come by to make my delivery." His cheeks reddened. "This week, however, Elbert wasn't expecting me. Vesta's thrown off my entire delivery schedule on account of this terrible situation."

"Vesta?"

"My wife," said Mr. Tidwell. He paused. "You'll meet her, I have no doubt." Heading toward the kitchen, he added, "But if you'll excuse me, Ms. Maitland, I've got to see a man about a fish."

Elsie smirked as he disappeared through the doorway.

The hotel manager's office was unfavorably small and smelt strongly of a cologne that held hints of deep-wooded musk, the result of Mr. Needling's overindulgent hand. There was just one window with which to air the room and it faced out toward the cliffs. The furniture was sparse and consisted of one desk, a single, narrow bookcase situated in the far corner of the room, and just two chairs: Mr. Needling's behind the desk and another in front. Today the hotel manager occupied the latter.

Sergeant Wilcox leaned against Mr. Needling's desk, considering the hotel manager thoughtfully.

"Mr. Needling," he began, "tell me what exactly you recall happening from a little before the time you heard the child crying."

"Well," started Mr. Needling, clearing his throat, "at about 10 pm I wrapped things up with our chef, Walton. Dinner had been served, the kitchen was cleared and Walton let me know that he was heading home."

"This is a typical end to the evening?"

"Oh yes," confirmed Mr. Needling. "So far everything seemed quite normal." He gave another short cough and went on. "Ms. Kemper, our maid, retired to her room soon after the cook left, just as I had done."

"Is your room near to hers?" asked Sergeant Wilcox.

"No, actually," replied Mr. Needling. "I take a room upstairs with the guests, at the far end of the hall. Ms. Kemper's is near the kitchen."

"Then what happened?" asked the sergeant.

"Well, it was a few hours later that everything started." Mr. Needling's small, dark eyes jumped about the room nervously. "First came the child's crying, which was quite strange since there was no child staying here at the hotel. Everyone rushed downstairs to figure out what was wrong. I went into Ms. Kemper's room to wake her, in hopes that she could help, but she wouldn't wake. Then the others arrived and seeing that the side door was open, we rushed out, thinking the child was in danger outside. But there was no child, just a tape recorder playing the *sound* of a child crying. Then Mr. James Rennick, one of the guests, called us to the reverend's room, where we found him dead!"

"And then someone discovered that the maid was, in fact, dead as well?"

Mr. Needling swallowed, licking his thin lips. "Yes, Mr. Paul Hulling discovered that to be the case."

"Do you know why anyone would want to kill either Ms. Kemper or Reverend Pennington?"

Mr. Needling shook his head adamantly. "Not at all," he gushed. "I'm dumbfounded by the whole thing!"

Sergeant Wilcox nodded, closing his notepad.

"Is there anything else, Mr. Needling, you can tell me for now?" he asked, standing.

"No, sir," replied Mr. Needling. "Not a thing."

It was just after lunch when Elsie entered the town's small florist shop. Behind the counter Mrs. Doris Malford smiled curiously as Elsie approached.

"Welcome," greeted the florist. "You must be new to our little town."

Elsie smiled.

"Yes, just visiting. I would like to place an order for two arrangements, please," she began, brushing her hand delicately across a beautiful crystal vase. "Something with soft whites and ivories, perhaps?"

"Of *course*. How I do love the simple elegance of whites and ivories." Mrs. Malford selected a few hydrangeas and added, "Is this for a wedding?" She seemed puzzled. "Although I haven't *heard* of any wedding."

Elsie lifted a rose to her nose. Shaking her head, she answered, "No, actually there are two people who have passed and I simply wanted to set out flowers in their memory."

Doris Malford's jaw dropped. "Norma and that... that reverend fellow, isn't it?!"

Elsie hesitated.

"Yes..." she started, slowly, "Reverend Pennington."

Mrs. Malford slid two planters across the counter, depositing a hydrangea into each. "Tell me what you know."

"*Excuse me?*"

Mrs. Malford sprinkled baby's breath haphazardly between the hydrangeas. "Did Vesta send you?"

"Vesta Tidwell?" asked Elsie.

"Oh! She *did* send you."

"No—no, I just..."

"How is her arm and leg? Still wrapped up in those casts, poor dear? Half her body out of order!"

"I have no idea about Mrs. Tidwell," explained Elsie. "I've only just heard her name from her husband—"

"An absolute dear the way he cares for her," gushed Mrs. Malford. "All of the town can't *imagine* how he puts up with her! Says that he can't possibly be happy being married to her, but *I* like Vesta just fine. And, wouldn't you know it, that poor husband of hers was just scared to death when his wife had that accident. She fell from a tree, you know. George—that's her husband—he was making deliveries when it happened. Left his route and went straight to the hospital, dear man." A placid smile swept across Mrs. Malford's face. "A testament to true love is what it is. Never even went back to his market. It's fish he sells."

Mrs. Malford paused, shaking her head admiringly.

"No, just rushed off and met his wife just as they were wheeling her into the ICU. That's the Intensive Care Unit."

"Yes, I'm familiar with the acronym, but *really* I only—"

Elsie jumped as Mrs. Malford smacked the palm of her hand atop the counter.

"But leave it to Vesta! Can't get around with that hopeless foot of hers, but she's sent a messenger." The florist mused, resting her face in her hands. "Do sit, dear," she motioned toward a stool. "Start from the beginning. What *happened?*"

"Look," demanded Elsie. "I—I don't know what you think, but *two* people's lives have been taken." She rested her arms squarely across her chest. "You want details of how it happened and why it happened, but the impression I get is that the 'who' doesn't seem to matter to you at all. But it matters to *someone*. And, if you ask me, they're the only ones that really need to know anything more about it."

She pulled a few stray hairs behind her ear and nodded toward the counter.

"Respectfully, will you make these arrangements, or do I need to take my business elsewhere?"

Mrs. Malford's face grew crimson as she stumbled back.

"I—I…"

She stood thoughtful for a moment, the palm of her hand pressed against her chest.

"I *really* don't mean to be rude," explained Elsie, "but it's out of respect for—"

Mrs. Malford lifted her hands. "Say no more, my dear," she began, her expression softening. "Yes. Yes, I would be very happy to make these flowers for poor Norma and the reverend."

Elsie's shoulders relaxed. "Thank you."

Mrs. Malford settled into her stool and gently arranged the baby's breath.

"Tell me," she began, peering curiously toward Elsie. "Have you had a chance to meet our friendly neighbors?"

"Not really. Only a few."

"Oh!" exclaimed Mrs. Malford, her excitement returning. "Let me tell you *all* about our little community!"

Elsie winced, forcing a reply.

"Yes, how nice…"

⧸⧹

Mr. George Tidwell returned home immediately from the hotel. Entering through his back door, he found his wife waiting eagerly for his arrival.

"Well?" demanded Mrs. Tidwell promptly.

He pushed aside his wife's novel and placed the empty fish basket on the nook table, near which she was still seated. She had waited with bated breath during the entire duration of his absence.

"I'm afraid, Vesta, that Sergeant Wilcox isn't telling *anyone* about anything at the moment," explained Mr. Tidwell.

Mrs. Tidwell snorted. "Impossible! He must tell the community something. It's only right!"

"Perhaps," agreed Mr. Tidwell, striding into the adjacent laundry room, "but *usually*, dear, the police do take some time to actually investigate things first."

Mrs. Tidwell pouted as her husband rummaged through a clean basket of clothes.

"So you really haven't found out *anything*, George?" she called.

A loud pot crashed just outside the kitchen window.

"Vesta!" yelled Mr. Tidwell, emerging from the laundry room. "Haven't I asked you to stop feeding those stray cats?" He tossed an apron over his shoulder. "They keep coming around here, trampling through my plants! You know I put a great deal of effort into my garden."

Mrs. Tidwell tugged sadly at her cast, prompting Mr. Tidwell to massage his temples.

"The only thing I heard…" he started.

Mrs. Tidwell beamed.

"…is that the murders might, just *might* have resembled the McCray murder from twenty years ago."

"Oh!" she exclaimed, her fingers gripping her chest. "What else?!"

"There really hasn't been *time* for anything else, Vesta. The sergeant had only begun to interview Dennis when I left, and all he had to say was that he was at the hotel the entire time everything happened." Mr. Tidwell shrugged. "You see, Vesta, it's all very disappointing. They haven't said anything more about the actual case."

"Mr. Needling?" asked Mrs. Tidwell, surprised. "The hotel manager said he was at the hotel?"

"That's right," confirmed Mr. Tidwell. "Where else would he be, dear? Now come along," he instructed, extending his hand. "I've got to get back to work and you'll be more comfortable on the couch."

Mr. Tidwell led his wife gingerly across the room.

"Where else indeed?" she murmured softly.

"Now, there you are, dear." Mr. Tidwell comforted his wife by pressing a pillow behind her back. "Can I get you anything else?"

She contemplated for a moment.

"Yes. I'll need the phone," she said decidedly.

Mr. Tidwell grimaced as he glanced at the time. Handing her the phone, he rushed toward the front door.

"Don't keep Doris too long!" he yelled, gripping his apron.

"But that *can't* be right," murmured Mrs. Tidwell.

She looked up to find that her husband had gone. Eagerly Mrs. Tidwell dialed the phone. On the second ring a man answered.

"Hello?" said Mrs. Tidwell. "Yes, may I please speak with Sergeant Wilcox?... Oh, I see. When do you think he will be back in?"

She listened intently.

"Yes, I understand... Conducting interviews is necessary, of course... A message? Yes, I think I should... Right, I'll hold."

A loud clatter came from the back porch once more.

"Those cats!" yelled Mrs. Tidwell as a voice murmured something on the other end of the line. "What's that?" she asked, returning her attention. "Oh, no! Sorry. Stray cats were making racket on my back porch. You ready? Yes, please ask the sergeant to come around to see Mrs. Vesta Tidwell as soon as possible... No, no. It's *Vesta*. Vesta with a 'V', as in *vigorous*... Good. Yes, that's right. Tell him that I really need to speak with him. It's very important. I've just realized something."

⁂

Still at the hotel, Sergeant Wilcox pulled out one of the chairs from the long wooden table in the kitchen.

"Walton, is it?" he asked.

Walton Schaeffer moved a skillet from the burner and turned off the heat.

"Yes, sir. I'm the chef here."

"And how long have you cooked at the hotel?"

Walton reflected for a moment.

"Coming on three years, sir. I like the work very much."

"I see." Sergeant Wilcox drew his pen. "And it is my understanding that you leave the hotel once you've finished dinner for the guests?"

"That's correct, sir." Walton pulled a checklist from the large freezer and handed it to the sergeant. "Besides preparing dinner, I make sure these tasks are done at the end of the evening as well. Norma would help with the dishes."

The sergeant nodded. "And tell me about Norma's mood yesterday. Did you notice anything unusual?"

Walton shook his head and leaned against the counter. "Not really. She served dinner, made minor mistakes here and there." He shrugged. "She wasn't the best maid I've ever worked with, but nice person. She wasn't upset or anything, if that's what you mean."

Walton paused.

"*Although*", he began, garnering the sergeant's full attention, "she did say she planned on moving up—and *out* of Westend Bay."

"Did she say anything else?" delved Sergeant Wilcox.

"She said she was tired of this small town. She wanted to go other places, but with her pay, I said, she couldn't afford it—not the places she was talking about, at least. New York, California… And that's when she said she planned on coming into some money soon. I had a dining room full of guests to cook for so I didn't stick around talking, but I did sort of wonder about it. Then again, it's Norma. She has always talked about wanting to move away from the small town life."

A knock came at the kitchen door.

"Sergeant Wilcox?"

The sergeant turned an impatient eye toward the officer in the doorway.

"I'm sorry to interrupt, but a message came for you from a Mrs. Vesta Tidwell. She asked for you to visit her, sir. She said she needs to tell you something important."

The sergeant grumbled before agreeing.

"Fine, I will see her next."

Chapter 5
MRS. TIDWELL

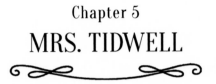

STEALING A GLANCE at his watch, Sergeant Wilcox rapped once more on the bright blue door of Mr. and Mrs. Tidwell's cottage. Again there was no response. The sergeant turned, intending to continue his inquiries elsewhere, but the faintest of cries coming from inside the cottage beckoned him.

"Hello?" he called.

Again there was no answer.

Turning the knob, the sergeant was only mildly surprised to find that the door was unlocked. *Old habits die hard*, he thought to himself, *even when there's a murder*. Slowly pushing the door open, he peered into the narrow hallway.

"Mrs. Tidwell?" he called.

He stepped his heavy boot into the foyer and advanced, listening intently for traces of the whimper he had heard before. With each step the hardwood floor groaned gently under his weight; small creases formed between the sergeant's eyes as he turned into the front sitting room.

He recoiled as he caught sight of a woman's leg stretched out across the floor, protruding from just beyond the couch, its ankle and calf wrapped in a cast and the foot resting limp in a pink, fuzzy slipper. A broken vase lay beside the slender leg.

The sergeant dragged his hands through his hair.

"No, it *can't* be. Not another one…" he murmured, stunned at the mere possibility of three deaths in such close proximity. He inched his way closer, but the sudden twitch of the woman's ankle made him jump.

"George?" murmured the woman softly. "Is that you? Are you here?"

The sergeant peered just beyond the coffee table and found Mrs. Tidwell helplessly prone on the floor, wedged between the couch and the end table. Bound in her casts, she flopped in tired bursts, like a fish on dry land—a fish that looked to Sergeant Wilcox like it was nearing its end.

Lifting her head, Mrs. Tidwell shouted out in surprise.

"Sergeant! How awful for you to find me this way! How this must look!"

The sergeant, although not fully recovered from his initial shock, pushed the table aside and reached forward to lift Mrs. Tidwell from the floor.

"Slowly… slowly now," she strained, gripping her shoulder.

"What in the world happened?" he asked.

Sinking into the floral patterned couch, Mrs. Tidwell waved her good hand wildly in the air.

"*Oh!*" she started, "I've had the most *trying* morning!"

Flushed, she tossed her head back onto a cushion before continuing.

"As you know I am terribly battered and bruised." She

brushed her hair back from her forehead. "Oh! That insufferable apple tree! Apples, Sergeant!"

"Apples, Mrs. Tidwell?"

"Apples," she stated definitively. "Apples have been the *bane* of women as far back as Eve! Apples!"

She reflected as she explained further.

"It was this morning that my dear husband, George, arranged my pillows and things down here on the couch. I was fine, so naturally he set off to work. That's when I called you."

The sergeant nodded.

"*Well*, I was quite comfortable until I suddenly realized that I had left the book I was reading on the kitchen table. So there I was, alone, and now I had this book on my mind. Tried to ignore it, I did. I *really* did." Mrs. Tidwell shook her head vigorously. "But you know how it is, Sergeant!"

Do I? The sergeant nodded noncommittally.

"Once you've started to think of the thing, you just can't get it out of your head! I've started this book and I *had* to know what happened next. All I could think about from that moment on was that there was a platinum blonde found dead in a library, face down on the floor!"

Mrs. Tidwell drew a startled breath.

"Oh... the *irony*," she purred.

Sergeant Wilcox sighed.

"And so you tried to reach for the book..." he encouraged.

"What's that?" Mrs. Tidwell regained her focus. "Oh!" She scratched absently at the top of her head. "Exactly! So I forced my way up and hobbled on my good ankle toward the kitchen. I tried to cut between the sofa and the end table, opting for the shortest route, and I slipped!" She collapsed backward into her pillows. "I got wedged between the furniture, unable to push myself up with my one good arm. Isn't that the most frustrating thing?"

"Mrs. Tidwell," started the sergeant slowly, "you pulled me away from a *murder* case to tell me something important."

"Oh, *yes*! It's all so sinister, isn't it?"

"*Why*, Mrs. Tidwell, did you call me?"

"Well, it's Mr. Needling. He is the reason I called."

"Mr. Needling?"

"That's right." Mrs. Tidwell shifted uncomfortably. "My husband tells me that Mr. Needling stated he was at the hotel all night, but I know for a *fact* that I saw him just after midnight creeping past my house. He was headed in the direction of the hotel with a package in his hand!"

"Really?" replied the sergeant with genuine interest.

"Yes!"

"Are you sure? Perhaps you could have been mistaken?"

"I'm positive," said Mrs. Tidwell adamantly. "I've got a street lamp just outside my window. I can never get comfortable with all these casts and it takes me eons to fall asleep, so you can see why a man walking down the street in the middle of the night would attract my attention."

"I do," agreed the sergeant.

"Now, as for poor Norma, Sergeant, what would you like to know?"

"Pardon?"

"Haven't you discovered?" said Mrs. Tidwell. "She worked here about twice a week. I've got what they'd call the 'inside scoop'!"

"Quite... I can imagine," he murmured. "Tell me, when was the last time you saw Ms. Kemper?"

Mrs. Tidwell considered.

"That would be a few days ago, just before she started work at the hotel. We've always been in agreement that when the hotel calls her with a larger assignment she is not expected to commit to her usual schedule with us—or any other residents, as far as I understand. She stays at the hotel for as long as they need her and then afterwards she returns to service individual homes as per usual."

"How long might she work at the hotel?"

Mrs. Tidwell debated.

"Anywhere from a few days to a couple of weeks at a time, if needed. They've got a small room there that she uses." She slapped her forehead and gasped. "I've just realized! What am I going to do without help around the house? I could handle going every now and again without Norma's help but imagine now—with my casts!"

Sergeant Wilcox cleared his throat. "But she didn't regularly work at the hotel?"

Mrs. Tidwell was puzzled for a moment.

"Oh! Norma?" She shook her head. "No, Mr. Needling only called her in when he anticipated several guests staying at the hotel—speaking of which, have you interviewed the millionaire couple yet?"

Sergeant Wilcox continued. "So, Mr. Needling *knew* he would have a larger number of guests than usual."

"I suppose so," replied Mrs. Tidwell. "Oh! Is *that* a clue?"

"And were you the only people, besides Mr. Needling, that Norma worked for?"

"Oh no, Sergeant! Norma kept her own schedule with several of the residents. One day here, two days there." She deliberated. "I know she worked for Dr. Linder, Mrs. Porter just down the road, and Doris…" She looked up. "That's Doris Malford, the florist."

"I see," replied the sergeant, noting the names in his pad. "And do you know any reason why anyone wouldn't like her? Would want her dead, even?"

"Nice girl overall, I think," stated Mrs. Tidwell, lowering her voice. "But Norma wasn't the most conscientious of workers. She was also a bit too *attentive* for my liking. And not to her work, I mean."

"You're saying she was nosy?" asked the sergeant bluntly.

"That's *exactly* what I'm saying. Just after I broke my arm and leg I asked her to pass my medicine bottle from the other room. She didn't know it, but I could see from the reflection in the mirror that she stopped to peer into one of our drawers! Of course, she closed the drawer as though she had done nothing wrong and handed me the medicine, but I know a nosy parker when I see one! I told Doris about it and she said she suspected Norma did the same thing at her house! Never took anything, mind you, but Doris and I agreed that there is nothing more *trying* than a nosy, busybody!"

The sergeant lifted one brow.

"Yes, thank you, Mrs. Tidwell."

❧ ❧

After finishing her shopping in town, Elsie Maitland settled in her room at the hotel. She scooted her chair forward at her desk and resumed writing the letter she had already started. Absently she dipped her hand into a can of cashews and reread all that she had already written. She still found it unbelievable that anyone would have been murdered, yet there was no denying it. Elsie exhaled and lifted her pen once more.

This morning I went to the local florist's (after having gotten the sergeant's permission, of course; after all, I am no doubt under suspicion!). The owner was something else, Franny! Complete gossip hound! In the time it took her to make my floral arrangements, she was able to get me up to speed on exactly who has done what and with whom. She told me about the gossip at the Empire Club—apparently a stuffy men's only establishment, yet she still seemed to know all the details—and I'm afraid that once the butcher catches wind of what the baker did last week, both will have lost each other as customers! Franny, I was certain she was going to slide a set of transcripts across the counter—all the neighbors' discussions documented and covertly folded into an empty seed packet!

You'll be happy to know, however, that I did (eventually) receive my two floral arrangements for Reverend Pennington and Norma Kemper. I just thought, I don't know… I suppose I just thought I should do something… and yet it still doesn't feel quite enough.

Elsie's pen hovered briefly over the page before she began writing again.

You know, Franny, I only had a brief conversation with Reverend Pennington, yet somehow I feel he has made a great impact on me. You know the type? A sincere man. It was something he said that really resonated with me: how we must "let justice roll down like waters. And righteousness like an ever-flowing stream."

Perhaps that is why the flowers don't quite seem enough? Reverend

Pennington came here for a reason—a reason that I suspect had to do with his murder. And that poor maid! I just don't know enough about what's happened. That brings me to my point.

I think I need to stay since I've got to find out. Just as you said.

A knock at the door startled Elsie.

"Ms. Maitland?"

Elsie rushed across the room in long strides to open the door.

"Mr. Rennick?" she replied with surprise. "I thought you might have been the police, or that something might have happened…"

James smiled as he looked at her expectantly.

"I'm sorry to trouble you, Ms. Maitland," he started, "but I thought perhaps we could talk?"

Elsie nodded. "Are you up for a walk?" she asked.

"That would be perfect."

⁓⳩ ⳩⁓

Dense, gray clouds shifted in front of the two o'clock sun as James and Elsie walked beside the hotel's cliffs, overlooking the sea. Although the top half of Elsie's long hair was clipped back away from her face, the rest lay just past her shoulders and danced wildly as a heavy, humid wind warned them of rain. Absently twisting her loose hair into an untidy bun, Elsie waved at Amos, who was further off in the distance, trimming a series of hedges to equal size. She laughed softly as the gardener nodded curtly and angled his body to face the other direction.

"You aren't… nervous?" asked James.

Elsie looked intently at James.

"Nervous?" she said, surprised. "About *you*, Mr. Rennick, or about being here?"

James smirked, casting a glance at his feet. "That's fair. Both, I suppose." He lifted his eyes; he too was amused. "I can see your point. *Someone* here has to be the killer."

Elsie pushed her glasses further up the bridge of her nose. She peered out toward the water, her nose gently rising and falling as she considered her response.

"It's uncomfortable, I admit," she remarked thoughtfully, "but I figure I don't know anything, so what would be the point of anyone hurting me?"

"Logical," he remarked, smiling. "But there are crazy people in the world. Perhaps our killer is not as logical as you are."

Elsie shook her head doubtfully. "Then why bother to arrange for these particular guests to be here at all? There is *some* sort of reasoning involved."

She took a seat atop a large stone.

"There it is again. Sound logic," repeated James.

Elsie shrugged.

"And that's why I wanted to talk to you," he said, lowering himself onto the grass beside her. "I've got a sort of proposition for you."

Elsie turned toward him in surprise. "What do you mean, 'proposition'?"

"I thought we could form a sort of partnership... in solving the case, I mean."

"What are we," she exclaimed, a smile tugging at her lips, "detectives?"

"Well, no—ok, maybe not *solve* it necessarily but find out what we can."

Elsie looked puzzled. "What's your interest in this, Mr. Rennick?"

"Please, call me James."

Elsie nodded, waiting.

"I'm a journalist," he answered. "I've got a breaking story here, but I can't be everywhere all at once. And, the way I figure it, you are the only one—besides me, of course—that isn't involved. You and I are both here by chance. So if we work together—"

"But why should I?" interrupted Elsie. "Not that you don't seem like a nice guy, but I don't know you."

"Right, this is true," admitted James. "But I am stuck here by accident just as much as you are. That should count for something. Remember, this was supposed to be a leisurely vacation for me."

"The prize you won?" asked Elsie.

"Right."

She mulled over the idea of his prize. "Puzzles."

"Excuse me?" asked James.

"This whole thing is a puzzle, or is it more like a game? Games, jokes, mischief, deception..." Elsie's nose twitched excitedly. "A trap... but for *whom*?"

"I'm sorry, what are you talking about?"

"Connections—it's how I think through things," she said, struggling to explain. "My mind takes in everything around me. What I mean is, even if pieces of information are all scattered, that doesn't change the fact that they are always still there in the back of my mind."

James's head tilted slightly to one side as he considered what she was saying.

"Places, people, what someone has said," added Elsie. "I

can, quite naturally, rearrange that information… and *connect* it together until it fits, like a puzzle." She waved her hand dismissively. "But the point is that I'm thinking of *your* puzzle."

"My puzzle?"

"Yes." Elsie turned a keen eye on James. "Has it ever occurred to you, James, that the prize you 'won' was *meant* to get you here just as much as everybody else?"

James stood. "What *do* you mean?"

"You told me a couple days ago that you don't even remember entering the contest, yet the prize happened to be a trip *here*."

"*Oh!*" James exclaimed, heat rising in his cheeks.

At James's shout, Elsie noticed Amos crane his neck in their direction and peer towards them with great suspicion. Huffing, he turned back toward his hedge, snipping forcefully and muttering under his breath.

"Sorry, I didn't mean to shout." James rubbed the back of his neck. "It just hadn't occurred to me, but you must see that it's ludicrous!" With his palms turned upward, he stressed: "I have absolutely *nothing* to do with these people!"

A faint drizzle greeted them.

"Will you help me?" asked James softly. "This time I'm asking for more reasons than just a news story. If—and I mean *if*—I am somehow drawn into this, I will need someone to help me. You're the only… outsider." He reassured her: "I'm not involved in any way."

Elsie deliberated.

"The sergeant," she began slowly. "He is working on—"

"No, it's not good enough."

James stretched out his hand toward the water.

"You see this town?" he exclaimed, pointing beyond

the cliff toward the rooftops of the small homes and shops. "Sergeant Wilcox has probably never even had a murder to solve! Just cats up trees and illegally parked cars."

"I suppose it wouldn't hurt to exchange ideas about things," she started. "But as for *solving* this, I'd like to, but I can't guarantee—"

"No, not even *solve* it, Ms. Maitland. Just think of it as helping the sergeant to… move things along."

Elsie stood.

"I was planning on keeping my eyes open anyway," she remarked, starting toward the hotel as the rain began to fall steadily. "I suppose it wouldn't hurt to exchange information."

"Good," said James, his stride falling a few steps behind hers.

"And perhaps", she said, looking over her shoulder, "you should call me Elsie—El for short."

⁓ ⁓

Dinner at the hotel started at half past six. Mr. Needling had yet to find a suitable replacement for Norma, so he was helping to serve dinner personally, and along with each dish he placed on the table, he offered a few reassuring words.

"All will be sorted out in no time," he said, depositing a steaming bowl of yellow rice beside James and the Hartwells.

"The sergeant is doing everything in his power to solve this terrible, *terrible* situation," he added, placing seasoned asparagus beside Paul, Elsie and Mr. Turnbull.

"I can't imagine it should take much longer," he went on as Mr. and Mrs. Welling considered the freshly placed platter of baked chicken.

"Mr. Needling," called Walton from the doorway, "Sergeant Wilcox is here. He needs to speak with you, sir."

Mr. Needling looked at his feet.

"Yes, of course."

He turned toward his guests.

"If you'll excuse me," he said, his ears reddening. "Please, enjoy your dinner."

With quick, small steps he took his leave.

"Could you pass the asparagus, please?" asked Marian, her voice just above a whisper.

"You all right, Marian?" asked Paul, handing her the bowl.

James's eyes followed Mr. Needling before casting a knowing glance at Elsie. Standing, he excused himself from the table and left the room. Elsie shifted in her seat.

"Right," she said.

Iradene Hartwell looked at Elsie, scrutinizing her closely.

"Perhaps," announced Elsie, clearing her throat, "perhaps we ought to have a discussion… about the murders."

There was a gasp as the bowl of asparagus crashed onto the table.

James crept down the hotel's empty hall, away from the dining room. Careful not to be seen, he rushed beyond the fireplace, dipping behind the front desk. He listened fixedly as he approached the manager's office door.

"Mr. Needling," Sergeant Wilcox addressed the manager firmly, "when I spoke to you earlier you informed me that you were here at the hotel the entire night the murders took place."

Especially intrigued, James carefully peered through a

tiny crack in the door. Mr. Needling was rubbing his hands together in small, unsteady circles.

"Yes, that's right." The manager loosened his tie.

"Interesting," replied the sergeant, leaning against Mr. Needling's desk. "I have it on good authority that you were actually *seen* the night of the murders coming down Shady Glen Road with a package in your hand."

Mr. Needling's face reddened.

"Would you care to explain, Mr. Needling?" The sergeant crossed his arms.

"I was afraid something would go wrong," Mr. Needling muttered, dropping his face into his hands. Then, lifting his head, he reached out his arms. "Ok, I *did* lie about having gone out last night, but it's not because I killed anyone, I swear. I only went out because I was instructed to do so…"

James tilted his ear closer to the door.

"I think you'd better explain," barked the sergeant.

"Right, of course." Mr. Needling licked his lips. "It started a few weeks ago. I received a call to book rooms, just like normal."

James drew back slightly as Mr. Needling cast his eye longingly toward the door.

"The man on the phone", he continued, turning back to the sergeant, "said he was making arrangements for several guests."

"Wait," interrupted the sergeant. "You're sure it was a man who called you?"

Mr. Needling seemed uncertain. "Well, no. I would say so, but then again… I can't swear to it. I didn't actually *see* the person."

"Go on," instructed Sergeant Wilcox.

"He gave me a list of names and said that he was arranging something special. Of course, I assumed it to be a sort of celebration, but he said no—a reunion. He didn't say much more beyond that; he was a bit secretive about everything. In fact, for a moment I considered just declining to make the arrangements. Something didn't seem quite right about it, but then he sent me cash to cover *every* guest, and a handsome tip! He said he would be in touch with further instructions. Until then I was simply to report to him if any of the guests *didn't* show. By that point I was more than willing to help. I mean, this is a *hotel*, after all, and I really don't *need* to know the details of why a guest is staying here."

"Did you initiate contact with any of the guests yourself, Mr. Needling?"

The manager shook his head. "I never spoke with any of the guests until they arrived. I was only told whom to expect."

"Did this man ask or say anything else—anything even remotely odd?" asked the sergeant.

Mr. Needling considered for a moment.

"The only thing that was odd, I suppose, was that he inquired about the other guests that were staying at the hotel, those who were not a part of his group. He wanted to know how many other guests would be here. Of course, I told him that I couldn't be sure. I book guests far in advance but also on the same day they arrive, as long as I have a room. In the end, though, he decided that it was all right—it didn't matter." Mr. Needling seemed puzzled. "Whatever that meant."

Sergeant Wilcox rubbed his chin thoughtfully. "And then he called you again the night of the murders?"

"That's right." Mr. Needling scooted forward in his seat. "He said he left a package with a tape recorder at the end of

Shady Glen Road, just inside the phone booth. I was to collect the recorder and play it by the cliffs in the middle of the night, at about half past two."

"And you didn't think it strange?" asked the sergeant.

"Well, of course I did!" exclaimed Mr. Needling. "But there was another wad of cash sitting in the box, and business isn't always *this* good. I thought, what harm could there be?"

"Two murders," replied the sergeant sharply.

"I *honestly* didn't know anyone was going to be murdered!"

"And where are your guests now?" asked Sergeant Wilcox.

"In the dining room. They should be finishing their dinner by now."

James backed away from behind the door and slipped quietly down the hall, returning breathlessly into the dining room. No one noticed him return, as a discussion was in full swing.

"I already told you all that I know!" yelled Mr. Welling. "I told you the first night I was here, for that matter!"

Olivia Welling slammed down her glass. "This is ridiculous!" she yelled, glaring at Iradene Hartwell from across the table. "Obviously someone has gone to a great deal of trouble to recreate the murder from twenty years ago! Why would you say it was Richard?"

"All right, everyone! Calm down." Elsie stood. "Ms. Hartwell, there's no point in making those types of accusations."

The older woman snorted as Elsie appealed to the group.

"We have come up with *some* helpful information, haven't we? There is at least one common thread we've uncovered so far."

"Skylark Travel Agency," said Mr. Turnbull, nodding. "A

company with which, might I remind all of you, *I* made no arrangements."

"Yes, your point is noted, Mr. Turnbull," replied Elsie. "The concern, however, is that there does appear to be an alarming number of guests who arrived after arrangements were made *for* them through this agency. Therefore, I think we ought to start there. We need to determine *who* made the arrangements. Certainly they must have a name on file."

"No one is going to leave a *name* if they are a murderer!" exclaimed Paul.

"Perhaps not," countered Elsie. "But maybe the person who took the call could tell us of any unusual mannerisms that the caller could have had, or perhaps whether it was a man or a woman."

"That *is* a start," mumbled Marian.

"We think we may be looking for a man."

Everyone turned swiftly toward the doorway. Sergeant Wilcox entered the room, his snout nose lifted high as he scanned the startled faces.

"A man, you say?" asked Iradene Hartwell.

"Perhaps," replied the sergeant. "Commendable suggestion, Ms. Maitland. However, we have already made a few inquiries into Skylark Travel Agency, as I too noticed that more than a few of you arrived through their services."

"*And?*" pressed Richard Welling.

"The name provided when making the arrangements was John Smith."

"Ha!" Paul threw up his arms. "What a joke!"

"We were able, however," continued Sergeant Wilcox, "to trace the calls back to a specific phone booth. In fact, he made several calls from this same location."

"A phone booth tells us nothing!" said Paul.

"On the contrary, the phone booth used is located at the train station—our very own Westend Bay platform."

"So it could be anyone going in and out of the station," said Iradene.

"*Or* it could be someone who lives near or in Westend Bay, which is my bet," countered the sergeant.

Olivia threw down her fork.

"Well, that narrows it down, doesn't it?" she scoffed, tucking her slick black hair behind her ear.

"Knowing *where* the calls were made, Mrs. Welling, gives us possible witnesses. It's just a matter of time. It's very likely we are looking for a local person." The sergeant sniffed and tugged at his belt. "I think you'll find that it's the *culmination* of information that matters, and that is why I'd like to continue my inquiries—starting with you."

Olivia's lips thinned.

Chapter 6
ELSIE AND JAMES

MRS. OLIVIA WELLING shivered in the cool room as she and her husband waited in Mr. Needling's office to be interviewed.

Mr. Welling took a seat beside his wife.

"I will just leave you to it, then," remarked Mr. Needling, closing the door on his way out.

Sergeant Wilcox strode toward the desk and slid a stack of Mr. Needling's papers to one side. Partially bearing his weight against the sturdy oak, he began his questioning.

"Mr. and Mrs. Welling would you please describe your whereabouts the night of the murders?"

Mr. Welling rested his elbows on his knees. "We've already described everything to that young officer of yours. No point in saying it all again, is there?"

"Perhaps," agreed Sergeant Wilcox. "However, we've taken the liberty of cross-referencing everyone's statements and there is something to do with yours that just doesn't quite add up."

Mr. Welling straightened. "Oh, is that so?"

The sergeant turned his gaze on Olivia.

"In your statement, Mrs. Welling, you indicated having followed your husband down the stairs in search of the crying child."

"That's correct."

"While others indicated that you announced you were going to retrieve your robe from your room and *then* meet the rest of the group below."

Olivia pulled back slightly in surprise.

"Well, I suppose I might have done so," she began slowly. She considered for a moment. "Yes. I did, actually... now that you mention it. I turned back to retrieve my robe and then immediately assisted the group in the search."

"But you didn't think to mention this?" asked the sergeant.

"What are you getting at, Wilcox?" demanded her husband.

"No, that's all right," interjected Olivia. "The reason I didn't say anything, Sergeant, is because I hardly recalled the fact myself. I didn't think something so trivial was worth mentioning. It couldn't have taken me more than a moment before I was with the others."

The sergeant crossed his arms.

"I see," he replied. "But the problem is that it would have only taken a moment—as you said—to hit Reverend Pennington over the head with a lamp."

Mr. Welling burst from his seat.

"I will *not* allow you to make any further defamatory remarks about my wife! She didn't even know this man and you would accuse her of bludgeoning him to death?! What is her motive then?"

"Calm down, Mr. Welling," replied the sergeant, now

standing. "I am simply trying to ascertain all the facts and consider *all* possibilities. And your point is valid."

Mr. Welling narrowed his eyes distrustfully. "Right," he murmured, clearing his throat. "And to which point might you be referring?"

"I would like to know whether your wife did know the reverend."

Sergeant Wilcox pointed his pug-like nose swiftly toward Olivia.

"*Did* you know Reverend Pennington, Mrs. Welling?"

"Oh!" Olivia clutched at her necklace. "No—no, of course not," she stammered.

Sergeant Wilcox snorted. "Never even seen him before?"

Olivia blushed.

"No," she stated. "Never in my life."

"Well," remarked the sergeant, "that must be a relief for you, Mr. Welling."

Mr. Welling made no reply. The sergeant smiled and walked slowly to the window, peering through it toward the cliffs.

"I don't intend to keep either of you much longer," he remarked, returning his eyes to the couple, "but if you would, Mr. Welling, could you tell me a bit about your former business partner, Mr. Edward McCray?"

Mr. Welling was slightly taken aback. "About Edward?"

"Yes, about the type of man he was. His character. Were you friends, for instance?"

Mr. Welling shook his head.

"No, I wouldn't say *friends*. He wasn't the type of man I'd fully trust, but I don't trust many people. I went into business with him because he had some strong connections. I always kept a discreet eye on his work though."

"Effectively?"

Mr. Welling grimaced.

"No, I'm afraid not. After he died I went over his affairs and discovered that he'd been syphoning money from one of our business accounts. Small amounts at a time—nothing you'd notice right away. It didn't ruin me. As you already know, our company bounced back without a hitch."

"And no one else knew about Mr. McCray dipping his hand in the till?"

Mr. Welling altered his posture.

"I'm sure someone else did," he said. "Once we found out about Edward's scheme it didn't take much effort for us to also determine that the money he took wasn't for his personal use."

"Blackmail," determined the sergeant. "He was trying to cover something up."

"The truth is", continued Mr. Welling thoughtfully, "both Edward and I tied up all of our money in the start-up of the company. He had his manor, of course, which was worth quite a bit, but no real liquid assets at that time, which is why I suspect he used his business account. If someone were blackmailing him for some personal reason he would have needed to gain cash quickly. I think his decision to steal from the company was just a means to an end." He scoffed. "Although, there is very rarely an 'end' with blackmailers."

Sergeant Wilcox readily agreed with his statement.

"Still, it didn't take long for the money to come rolling in," continued Mr. Welling. "Had Edward not died he would have been able to pay back the money he took from the business tenfold, and since the withdrawals weren't substantial enough to draw a red flag I probably never would have known about it, as long as he put it back before our next audit! Really, I expect that's what he planned to do. Either way, the business was obviously a success and, as per our contract, Edward's wife benefited, receiving a substantial amount of return for her husband's role in starting the company."

Placing his hands in his pockets, Sergeant Wilcox asked, "Do you know who was blackmailing him, Mr. Welling?"

"I can't prove it, but I'm pretty sure."

Sergeant Wilcox leaned in. "Oh?"

Mr. Welling responded with asperity.

"That vindictive bat—Iradene Hartwell."

<hr/>

With all the happenings and activity in the hotel, Elsie found it necessary to head outside. As she spread a blanket across the damp grass, she looked out onto the water and listened to the waves crashing into the cliff. The sound of footsteps distracted her from her respite; she turned to find James approaching from behind.

"It feels like the temperature might drop tonight," he called. "But at least the rain has stopped."

Elsie smiled. "I don't mind. I love the breeze and the waves."

James stepped beside her. "Interesting dinner," he said, smirking.

"*Very.*"

He patted his pant pockets. "Haven't come across an old address book, have you?"

"No, I'm sorry. Lost yours?" she asked.

"Yes. I tend to do that, though."

Elsie grinned. "Me too."

"Of course," added James good-humoredly, "it usually shows up days later—only *after* I've already tapped into my extraordinary journalistic skills to find the numbers I needed. It's all really just an enormous waste of energy."

Elsie smiled, peering out toward the darkening sky with hues of yellow, orange and red painted above it in masterful strokes.

James hesitated.

"Are you—may I... join you?"

Elsie gathered her wrap to her sides. "Please. You're not too cold?"

James shook his head. "I never did get cold easily. Even as a child my parents had to force me to wear my jacket when I'd go out to play. Of course, I always took it off when they weren't looking." He wound his shoulder. "It restricted my throwing arm."

Elsie teased. "And at that age you were undoubtedly an all-star."

"Right you are, my lady."

A series of lights flickered on, surrounding the perimeter of the hotel.

"The sun's almost down," James remarked.

Now more pensive, he rested his weight on his elbows.

"Why are you here, amidst all this madness?" he asked, turning his head toward Elsie.

"You mean besides the fact that Sergeant Wilcox would probably hunt me down if I left?"

"Precisely."

Elsie smiled gently. "I guess... justice. I would like to see justice done for the reverend and Norma... And also," she reflected, "I'm also here for my sister."

James rolled onto his side. "It's nice that you're close to your sister. I don't have any siblings."

"How about your parents?" asked Elsie. "Are you close to them?"

James considered for a moment. "I am, actually."

He smiled contentedly as the steady rhythm of the waves crashed below and heavier gusts of wind met them above the cliffs. Elsie drew her wrap tighter around her shoulders.

"You're still all right without a jacket?" she asked.

James smiled up at her. "I'll be fine, but thanks."

She stilled. "You've got a scar," she remarked as the wind parted his hair. She brushed a finger above her eye, indicating the area of which she spoke.

"*Oh*," started James. "Just a small accident when I was younger—don't even remember it." He tousled his hair. "It's why I go for the intentionally messy look." He grinned, his eyebrows jumping up and down.

Elsie laughed as she turned back toward the sea.

"If you don't mind me asking, what happened in the jet-skiing accident with your sister?"

"A little over a year ago Frances took a vacation. She'd gone rock climbing, sailing—all that sort of exciting stuff. So naturally jet skiing was a must. She was going full speed around a small island. She cut through a narrow inlet, but there were several tall trees so she couldn't really see too far ahead. Unfortunately a fishing boat was motoring through from the other direction. There wasn't much room for either of them. She tried to cut a sharp turn to avoid hitting the boat, but she couldn't manage it. There was very little option as to where she could go."

Elsie picked at a few blades of grass beside her.

"She's fine overall," she continued, "but the accident did a number on her legs and hip. She is using physical therapy to help get her walking again. She will get there, but it will take some time."

"And what about you?" asked James, his expression thoughtful.

Shaking the grass from her fingertips Elsie laughed, surprised. "What about me?"

"Are you as adventurous as your sister?"

She chuckled.

"Hardly," she replied quietly, staring down at her hands. "Really it was my sister who suggested I visit a town near here so I could try rock climbing. Honestly, I agreed because I wanted to live fully for the both of us, since Frances can't do what she enjoys right now…"

Her voice trailed away.

"But is that what you want to do?" James asked.

Elsie immersed herself more snugly in her throw and turned her body toward James.

"There is something I've only just come to realize," she started slowly. "Frances has always been the more adventurous one. In our family she has always been the one that's so full of life and, I guess, after thirty years I got into the habit of stepping back, if that makes sense. Somewhere along the way I settled into the sort of comfortable, quiet approach to life." She reflected. "But with Frances getting hurt, the dynamic has changed a bit… *She* used to be the one that would talk a little louder or laugh a little harder, and now, without her doing that, I guess I've only just realized how safe and quiet I've become. And for the first time I'm wondering if I've been too safe? Too quiet?"

James sat up and listened closely.

"I mean, I own a wonderful little bookstore, which I love," she continued, "but after I close up shop for the day, I finish whatever book I'm reading and climb the steps to my apartment, which is just above the store!" She laughed. "I *literally* live in a world surrounded by amazing, exciting stories... but none of them are mine."

James inched just a little closer to Elsie and focused his eyes on hers.

"Maybe..." he began, pausing briefly as he collected the right words. "Maybe," he started again, gently placing her hand in his. "You should step into something you never would have done before. Just maybe it's time to be a bit bolder." He smiled. "I think that when you go after something you desire, even when the journey ahead scares you a bit, *that's* when you define what 'adventurous' means for *you*. Be *Elsie* bold," he added, flashing a lopsided grin.

They both turned back toward the sea and sat in silence.

"James..." she said, still peering ahead. "Thanks."

"You're welcome, Elsie."

Slowly a grin spread across her face. "I suppose one *really* hasn't lived until they've been a part of a murder mystery, has one?"

James laughed.

"No, Elsie, they haven't," he agreed. "You're off to an amazing start... mysteries," he murmured, shaking his head thoughtfully. "*Oh... mysteries!*" He threw up his arms. "I can't believe I didn't tell you right away!"

"Tell me what?"

"Apparently Mr. Needling was actually *paid* to play the recorder with the child's cry," he whispered intensely.

"You're kidding!"

James looked over his shoulder.

"He knew about the guests but claims not to know why they were all called here. He said he received instructions that a package with a tape recorder was going to be delivered at the end of Shady Glen Road, just inside the phone booth. He was to pick it up and play it about half past two. Of course, you know what happened next." James's face grew grim. "Mr. Needling *also* said he didn't know anyone was going to be murdered, but you wouldn't expect him to say anything else, would you?"

"No," murmured Elsie. "So Mr. Needling is either lying and did actually plan all this—but we still have no reason as to why—*or* he is telling the truth and he was just a pawn. Someone used him to help recreate the murder from twenty years ago..."

"My bet is on the latter," said James. "Mr. Needling is a bit... odd, let's say, but I don't see him planning all of this."

"No, I agree," said Elsie. "I don't either."

⁓⸪⸪⁓

Later that night, Elsie was settled in her room half way through writing another letter.

So that's all I know Mr. Needling has admitted so far, Franny, she wrote.

Elsie shook her pen when it suddenly stopped working. Rising from her bed, she dug through her bag for another. Snack crackers, receipts, a dog collar and a wallet tumbled out, but no pen.

"Oh bother," she murmured. "*How* did that get in here?" She lifted the dog collar curiously. "It's like everything has legs," she said, tossing it back into her purse.

She headed to her writing desk and searched through the drawer. Finally finding a pen, Elsie lifted her head only to catch a glimpse of something moving outside her window. Curious, she focused on a shadowy figure of a man walking hurriedly across the hotel's lawn.

"Who would be out this late?" she questioned, looking at the time. "Half past eleven."

She looked again and found the man's figure disappearing down the driveway into town. Stretching, she climbed back into bed. Lifting the letter, her lips moved silently as she reread what she had last written.

"Right—Mr. Needling..." she recalled aloud. She pressed her pen against the stationery and began again.

Really, Mr. Needling could be more deeply involved than he says, but a hunch tells me he's not. I suppose I will go with that for now. James seems to think so too...

Elsie paused, biting gently on her bottom lip before continuing.

I haven't told you much about James Rennick, have I?

She rested her pen to her cheek and considered her letter carefully.

"Live life," she uttered softly to herself as she started writing again.

James and I have sort of become allies in this tragic event, and yet I wonder if there is such a thing as an ally—in cases of murder, I mean. Really, Franny, I can't trust anyone, can I? And yet I have to trust someone, right? It's all a bit bewildering. I can't imagine that James could be involved. I know it sounds ridiculous—just like what characters in your books would say right before they are shot with the revolver or bludgeoned on the head—but he really does seem trustworthy! May I disgust you further? He sort of reminds me of a sleepy beagle with tousled hair. You know, he has <u>honest</u> eyes. Ha!

THUMP! That was the sound of a man—with honest eyes—sneaking up behind me, swinging a blunt instrument toward my head.

In all seriousness, though, it's hard to tell if it's me just being silly or if maybe I ought to trust my instincts… but I'm afraid because they've never really been tested.

I've thought about what you said—you know, find out about the child and the mom. It could be any number of people here, if you think about it. There is Mr. Paul Hulling, James Rennick, and the now wealthy Mrs. Olivia Welling. Oh! I should tell you. Apparently Mrs. Olivia Welling was raised only by her mother—just like Mrs. McCray, who left Westend Bay with her child. Really, any of them could be the McCray child! I suppose I need to strike up 'casual conversation' with each and see what I can find out.

Elsie thought for a moment.

Something is nagging at me, but I can't recall exactly what. Perhaps if I don't think about it, it will come to me.

Franny, I wish you were here. You would probably see things more

clearly. I will keep you posted as more develops. Tell Lawrence thanks
again for watching my little store.

Love you lots

—El

P.S. I finally found Hubert's collar in my purse. No, I don't know how I
managed it.

⚜

In spite of all the discussion pertaining to the investigation, Iradene Hartwell seemed unusually hushed, yet Sergeant Wilcox was determined to uncover more. A uniformed officer followed Ms. Iradene Hartwell into Mr. Needling's office.

"Ms. Hartwell."

The sergeant greeted her as he turned from the office window. The officer nodded to Sergeant Wilcox as he took position behind his superior.

"Your officer said you wanted to speak with me?" said Iradene.

"Yes, please. Have a seat," replied the sergeant. He looked toward the door. "Your sister is not joining us?"

"She's expressed that she is not feeling well. Now, may we proceed? I have far better things to do with my time."

"Very well," agreed Sergeant Wilcox amiably. "Let's cut to the chase, Ms. Hartwell. We have reason to believe that twenty years ago you were involved in blackmail. More specifically, you were the blackmailer."

Iradene neither looked surprised nor upset by this accusation. She replied, "That's amusing, Sergeant, but I have never been nor would I ever fall on the wrong side of the law. I have no need. I'm quite a wealthy woman in my own right. In short, I don't blackmail plebeians."

The sergeant's lip curled. "How thoughtful of you."

Officer Jenkins grumbled his disapproval under his breath.

Iradene stood. "Now if there's nothing else—"

"Please take a seat, Ms. Hartwell." The sergeant's voice was firm. "I'm not done."

Iradene hesitated. Lifting her chin, she complied.

"Tell me, Ms. Hartwell, how did you know Mr. Edward McCray?"

"Through business acquaintances."

"So you were not personally close to him or his family?"

Iradene twisted her face in disgust. "Of course not."

"Then why did you feel compelled to come back to Westend?"

"I received a letter that threatened to tarnish my name. Naturally I wouldn't allow such a thing."

"Tarnish *your* name?" The sergeant smirked; a sharp sniff came from behind his shoulder. "From what my officers and I have uncovered so far, Ms. Hartwell, your name couldn't be more infamous if you tried, so tell me another one."

"There is no need," she hissed. "My lawyer arrives in town tomorrow and you can take this matter up with him."

Iradene stood, but this time she did not stay.

The officer stepped forward. "So what do you think?" he asked.

"She's a liar."

Chapter 7
WHILE AT DR. LINDER'S OFFICE

DR. CHARLES LINDER'S office, although sparsely furnished, was most welcoming given the friendly staff. Inside the first exam room Mrs. Vesta Tidwell scooted forward on the thin paper that stretched across the pale green exam table.

"Now how does that feel, Mrs. Tidwell?" asked Dr. Linder as he conducted his exam.

Mrs. Tidwell made a slight grimace as Dr. Linder gently lowered her arm to her side.

"Just a bit stiff and a little strange not having the casts on, but overall it feels fine, I'd say."

Dr. Linder nodded. "It will feel that way for a while."

"So tell me, Dr. Linder, what have you uncovered on the autopsy reports concerning poor Norma and that poor, dear reverend?"

Dr. Linder sighed.

"I'm not the attending physician on the case, Mrs.

Tidwell." He lifted her leg gently. "Therefore, I have no information on the matter. As far as your recovery," he continued, lowering her leg approvingly, "both your arm and leg haven't been utilized for quite some time. You'll feel quite weak in both. I will put you in touch with a physical therapist."

"Oh! That's *right*! You're a *suspect*…"

Visibly irritated, he ignored her remark and continued to provide plans for her treatment.

"I will provide a prescription for the pain," he explained, scribbling across his notepad. "And, of course, make sure to do your physical therapy. I'm serious, Mrs. Tidwell," he said, tearing the small, square sheet from its pad. "Don't go running around town just yet—you'll hurt yourself."

"But I—"

"*Mrs. Tidwell.*"

Defiant, her small nose crinkled forward.

"Dr. Linder," she stated poignantly, "I don't think you understand the gravity of your request. I've been housebound for *weeks* during the most exciting time in Westend Bay's history, with the exception of the murder twenty years ago, of course. My husband is of absolutely no help as far as gathering information, and I can only be sure of what's really going on if I investigate matters myself! Do you understand?"

Dr. Linder opened the exam room door. "If you'll excuse me, Mrs. Tidwell, I need to retrieve the cane you will have to use until your physical therapy is complete."

"*Cane*?!" she huffed as he closed the door behind him.

Dr. Linder soaked in a few moments of silence as he massaged gently at his temples.

"Dr. Linder, good morning."

The doctor turned, startled. He saw a middle-aged man of

average height with stooping shoulders and a good-humored face.

"I'm Dr. Joseph Harrison," the man continued, extending his hand. "I am the chief pathologist concerning the Pennington and Kemper murders."

"Of course! Yes, yes," Dr. Linder nodded in recollection. "It's a pleasure to meet you."

"I apologize for interrupting your busy schedule," remarked Dr. Harrison. "But since you are Ms. Kemper's primary care physician, I felt compelled to notify you of my findings."

The door to the exam room quietly crept open as Mrs. Tidwell peered through the narrow crack. Her dark, brown eyes shifted left toward the front door as it chimed, revealing Sergeant Wilcox.

"Dr. Harrison, I was told I could find you here," greeted the sergeant. He nodded toward Dr. Linder. "Doctor."

"Good timing," remarked Dr. Harrison. "I was just about to discuss my findings with Dr. Linder."

Moving toward the front desk, Dr. Harrison drew a leather-bound notebook from his jacket pocket.

"I think you will consider my findings of great interest," he began.

Mrs. Tidwell flinched as she shifted her weight uncomfortably onto her bad leg. Her determination, however, was unwavering. Leaning appreciatively against a cabinet near the door, she set her eyes firmly on Dr. Harrison.

He continued: "The finding as to the cause of the reverend's death is not particularly surprising."

Dr. Linder crossed his arms and gave a sharp nod. "A blow to the back of the head."

"That's correct," confirmed Dr. Harrison. "The base of the

lamp was indeed the weapon. Forensics has confirmed a match from the blood."

"Probably didn't know what hit him," muttered the sergeant.

"That brings us to the maid…" Dr. Harrison reviewed his notes. "Yes, Ms. Norma Kemper." He lifted his head. "Cause of death: white snakeroot."

"White *what?*" asked Sergeant Wilcox.

"White snakeroot. It's an extremely toxic herb with clean, white petals. It looks harmless enough—at least to a layman— but the plant contains a toxin called tremetol, primarily found in the leaves and stems."

"But when?" muttered Dr. Linder. "When would the toxin have been administered? It must have been something she ate, but to my knowledge all the guests had the same thing."

Dr. Harrison added: "It might help to know that this herb can kill in one large dose, but it can also kill over a period of time."

"So you're suggesting she was given multiple smaller doses?" considered Dr. Linder. "Yes, that would make sense."

"What are we talking about here, Doctor?" interjected the sergeant. "She takes these herbs a little at a time and then suddenly just keels over?"

Dr. Harrison closed his notebook. "It's more likely that her health was deteriorating while she unwittingly consumed the drug, but her symptoms were not so severe initially. I expect that she displayed any number of vague symptoms—sweating, shallow respiration perhaps. She might have simply dismissed it as something minor, such as the onset of a cold. Unfortunately the cumulative effect of the herb can ultimately result in heart failure—and death."

Elsie walked down the steep gravel drive from the Hotel Westend as she headed into town. Gripping the railing, she turned toward the sea and inhaled the moist, salty air and the familiar scent of seaweed that drifted up from the jagged rocks below. She watched the low, gentle morning tide as its waves warmly greeted the shore. She took pause, however, when she noticed a set of footprints imbedded in the sand, disappearing beyond a small bed of rocks. Curious, she descended further down the drive; bits of gravel rolled out from under her heel as she crouched down.

"A tackle box," she murmured quietly, squinting as glare from the sun fell across her eyes.

Blinking past the brightness Elsie spotted the end of a fishing rod protruding from a small cavity in the cliffs. She could hear voices, but from her position her vision was blocked by several boulders. She wrapped her hand tightly around the railing and inched further out, a little over the cliff's edge, peering once more toward the small cavern.

At the other end of the fishing rod was Mr. Elbert Turnbull and beside him was a stocky man with an equally thick beard.

"They're not biting much," murmured Mr. Turnbull, reeling his fishing line toward him as his eyes focused on the bobber bouncing against the waves.

Elsie focused her eyes, imagining the bearded man as a shadow. She skimmed his frame and his gait as he paced beside Mr. Turnbull. *Yes*, she thought, *that's the man I saw crossing the lawn last night.* The man affixed his tired, puffy eyes onto Mr. Turnbull.

"Where is he now?" the man asked.

Mr. Turnbull spoke from the side of his mouth. "Inside the hotel, as far as I know. He was there not more than half an hour ago."

The man rubbed his fingers through his beard as he continued to pace slowly in the small space. "How could this have happened?" he hissed, turning back toward Mr. Turnbull.

Mr. Turnbull gestured for his acquaintance to lower his voice as he pulled his eyes sharply from his fishing line. "You're asking *me?*"

The bearded man was silent for a moment then decided, "We've just got to get him out of there. You're going to have to strike up a conversation with him, draw him out to me."

Mr. Turnbull's face grew grim as he debated.

"That's fine," he finally agreed. "Seems simple enough. I'll think of some reason."

"When?"

"A little before dinner," said Mr. Turnbull. "Everyone is usually back at the hotel by then. What I'll do is mee—"

"Ms. Maitland!" called a voice from behind her.

Elsie jumped, knocking her side into the railing. Wincing, she pulled her body back through the gap toward the drive. Rubbing her shoulder, she straightened and found an older woman with frizzy gray hair and a cane lumbering toward her.

"Ms. Maitland!" called the woman once more.

Elsie cut a sharp look toward the rocks below. Mr. Turnbull must have heard them, as he was hastily fumbling with the tackle box, motioning for the bearded man to leave in the other direction. Rubbing her ribcage, Elsie sighed and turned her attention to the stranger who knew her name.

"Ms. Maitland, isn't it?" huffed Mrs. Tidwell heavily, resting her weight against her cane. "Are you Ms. Elsie Maitland?" she asked again.

"That's right," Elsie replied cautiously. "Do I... Have we met?"

"Oh!" Mrs. Tidwell threw back her arm, laughing boisterously as she rocked unsteadily against her cane. "No, of course we haven't, have we?! But I know *you*!"

She pressed a wrinkled finger against Elsie's shoulder. This statement, however, did not prove to be reassuring to Elsie in the least.

"But, oh!" exclaimed Mrs. Tidwell. "You *should* know me—had I not been housebound and restricted by those miserable casts! *Absolute* torture, it's been! *Weeks*, Ms. Maitland." She tilted her head forward. "*Weeks*."

"I'm sorry to hear that," said Elsie.

Mrs. Tidwell went on. "Thank God for Doris or I'd know nothing! *Absolutely* nothing! She told me about you, of course. Came in to see me the day after..." Mrs. Tidwell lowered her voice, "...the *murders*."

"Right, well—" started Elsie, inching to her right.

Mrs. Tidwell shifted right as well.

"*And* to think that such a young, beautiful thing as you should be mixed up in such a sordid affair!" Mrs. Tidwell pressed her hand to her chest. "I knew you right away, I did. Doris described you exactly! Just like Dorothy Dandridge but with that fancy French braid that sort of wraps around to the side." Mrs. Tidwell leaned to one side, her hand hovering over her hair. "Oh! And you wear those large spectacles!"

Elsie's eyes widened.

"That must be popular now, is it?" asked Mrs. Tidwell,

waving her finger across her eyes. "To emphasize one's visual impairments?"

"I…" Elsie puzzled for a moment before finally managing to reply. "Ma'am, I'm glad to see you out and about, but—"

"Mrs. Tidwell, Vesta Tidwell."

"What's that?" Elsie's brows drew together.

"My name," stated Mrs. Tidwell. "It's what you wanted to know, I'm sure!"

Elsie lifted her shoulders.

"You must have met my husband, George? The local fish salesman, delivers fish around town, and delivers them *here*…" encouraged Mrs. Tidwell, "…to the hotel."

"Yes! Of course," replied Elsie honestly. "It's been wonderful, but I think—"

"So, there I am in bed," continued Mrs. Tidwell, sticking out her cane as Elsie maneuvered left. "Can't get around without an able-bodied person to hoist me about the place and then *this* happens!" She gazed at the hotel. "Murder," she muttered dreamily.

"I've got to go," stated Elsie firmly.

"But I wonder why white snakeroot, Ms. Maitland…" Mrs. Tidwell's gaze fell back onto Elsie. "Strange, don't you think?"

"I have no idea *what* you're talking about, Mrs. Tidwell." Elsie carefully steered her body past the woman. "Now if you'll excuse me."

"That's what Norma was killed with: *white snakeroot*."

Elsie stilled and turned around to find Mrs. Tidwell's head perched to one side, deliberating on the matter.

"It *is* strange, isn't it?" considered Mrs. Tidwell further, "To kill poor Norma that way."

The older woman straightened, shifting her weight.

"You said it was white snakeroot?" asked Elsie.

Mrs. Tidwell nodded excitedly. "An herb, apparently. Kills over time. Well, at least it did with Norma. Doctors said it *could* have been all at once, but it wasn't."

"And the doctors actually told you this?" asked Elsie doubtfully.

"Ha! Of course not, dear! No one ever *voluntarily* tells you anything. You've got to listen for it!"

Their conversation was punctuated by footsteps from above. Elsie looked past Mrs. Tidwell and noticed Mr. Needling appear at the top of the drive, his hands filled with stamped envelopes.

"Ms. Maitland," he greeted. His eyes widened at the sight of Mrs. Tidwell. "And Mrs. Tidwell," he said, his tone guarded.

His eyes trailed the length of Mrs. Tidwell's previously broken arm and leg, noting that she was very much free from her casts.

"Oh, dear," he murmured.

"Might you help me up to your hotel, Mr. Needling? I need to… catch my breath."

Mr. Needling's shoulders drooped.

"Of course, Mrs. Tidwell. Right this way."

⁙

As Mr. Needling escorted Mrs. Tidwell to the hotel, Mr. Turnbull was already in his usual location in the lobby. Sinking into the wingback chair, he sipped contemplatively from his drink and closed his eyes.

This whole business is a mess—a terrible mess. He pressed the cool glass to his lips, finishing off the liquor. *You would think that twenty years later, you'd be safe from it all...*

The sound of the hotel's front door opening resonated throughout the lobby.

"Oh! Here is *just* fine, Mr. Needling!"

Mr. Turnbull's eyes shot open.

"Hello, Elbert!"

"Mrs. Tidwell," murmured Mr. Turnbull darkly. He pushed a stack of old newspapers to the side and rested his empty glass on the table. "You've been... released."

"Ah!" Mrs. Tidwell fell back into the adjacent chair. "I got my casts off today, you mean?"

Mr. Turnbull looked at her without replying as she continued.

"Yes! And, of course, I came straight here!"

She raised a weary hand to her forehead.

"Where's Walton?" she called over her shoulder. "I need some water. That hill! It will be the death of me!" She dug into her purse. "Where are those pills the doctor gave me?"

"Mrs. Tidwell," grumbled Mr. Turnbull. "Shouldn't you be at home? Resting, perhaps?"

"Oh! Nonsense!" Mrs. Tidwell waved her hand, two pill capsules pinched between her fingers. "Mr. Needling!" she called, craning her neck toward the front desk. "I'll be in need of a room for the night. Could you notify my husband?" She fell back into her chair as Walton deposited a glass of water beside her. "I can't keep straining myself on these hills." She shook her head and tossed both pills into her mouth.

Mr. Needling sighed from behind the front desk as he dialed the phone. Mrs. Tidwell leaned forward and reached toward the table.

"Any of these papers from today?" she asked.

Mr. Turnbull sighed, closing his eyes in a thoroughly dissatisfied manner.

"No, they're not," he replied.

"Oh, what's *this*?"

Mr. Turnbull peeked cautiously through one eye. Mrs. Tidwell was examining a small, black book.

"*Oh*, an *address* book."

She scooted back into her chair.

"Now I wonder whose this could be," she whispered excitedly as she turned through the pages.

Mr. Needling held the phone against his chest. "Your husband requests that you return home, Mrs. Tidwell."

"Nonsense!" she exclaimed, turning to the 'G' tab. "Tell him it's already been settled. No, better yet, tell him my body is in a great deal of pain and it wouldn't make any sense to put any more strain on it this evening," she added, continuing to flip through each page. "Yes, he will agree to that."

Mr. Turnbull groaned as Mr. Needling complied with her request.

"I thought you might be in need of this, sir."

Mr. Turnbull's eyes fluttered open to find Walton offering him a glass of brandy.

"For the… shock, sir."

"Bless you, Walton."

"Oh!" exclaimed Mrs. Tidwell, lifting her head. "*Oh!*"

Mr. Turnbull groaned more deeply and took a hearty sip of his drink.

"The—the name here!" Mrs. Tidwell's gaze lingered in the 'P' section of the address book as she jabbed her finger repeatedly against the page.

"Calm down, Mrs. Tidwell," soothed Walton as the hotel's front door opened.

Elsie entered, slowing her gait as she came upon Walton; he was hunched over Mrs. Tidwell, whose chest was rising and falling heavily.

"Mrs. Tidwell!" called Elsie, running toward the chairs. "Is she all right?"

"She seems to have been excited by something," he replied. "Slow down, Mrs. Tidwell. Please, just say what you need to say. Take your time."

"Reverend Pennington," murmured Mrs. Tidwell. She pointed once more to the address book. "His contact information is *here*. And beside his name it says 'meet at HW'. *HW*. That must mean the *Hotel Westend*."

Curious, Elsie peered over Walton's shoulder. "What's that you're reading?"

"That's just it," said Mrs. Tidwell. "It's *Mr. Rennick's* address book."

Elsie straightened. "*James* Rennick?"

Mrs. Tidwell nodded, pointing once more toward the page. "*He* knows the reverend, and he made plans to meet him *here*…" She held her breath in an excited silence.

"And then the reverend *died*," murmured Walton. "I suppose we should call Sergeant Wilcox," he added, glancing uneasily between Mr. Turnbull and Elsie.

Mr. Turnbull took another long, steady drink of his brandy.

Chapter 8
JAMES IS QUESTIONED

HAVENFIELD WAS A mid-sized town that consisted not only of a bustling inner city—that featured an array of small shops, beautiful parks and even its own first-rate museum—but also beautiful countryside just on the outskirts. The latter was where Frances Maitland, having always been partial to the tranquility offered by wide, open lands, built her home.

It was here, in the comforts of her bedroom, that Frances reviewed Elsie's most recent letter with both concern and intrigue. Sitting on a long, white bench situated in the warmth of her bay window, she nibbled absently on a coconut drop as her physical therapist, Bernadine Eppler, entered with a black and white pug traipsing eagerly behind her.

"It's time for your exercises, Ms. Franny," announced Bernadine, whose voice was perpetually settled among the higher registers, a startling quality to which Frances had only recently become accustomed. Where the tone of Bernadine's voice was high, her body was similarly wide. She wore gray scrubs with white trim which was in considerable contrast to her curly, auburn hair. Although piled high on the center of her head, her hair was known to gradually favor one side by the day's end.

"Are you writing again?" asked Bernadine, stunned.

Frances's desk was the focal point of her room, but since the accident it had tragically not been used. Today, however, there were several sheets of paper scattered across the top of what Frances had come to affectionately call her 'old friend'.

"I felt… inspired," replied Frances, a placid smile crossing her lips.

With the exception of her antique writing desk, Frances' room, painted in a traditional, warm blue, was offset by pieces of classic, mahogany, eighteenth-century reproduction furniture. A bookshelf lined the far wall and was full to capacity, which accounted for the stacks of books that formed in various and often impractical spots on the floor. It was one of these stacks with which Bernadine was presently contending. Cautiously she maneuvered Frances's walker between the books and the mystery writer's treasured desk.

"Bernie!" exclaimed Frances, tossing back the bangs that swept over one eye, a gesture which had quickly become habit as a result of her recent shorter hair style, a chic pixie cut. "I've got updates for you."

Frances arranged Elsie's letters in date order and spread them out across the bench beside her. Having not yet received his proper greeting, Hubert, Frances' eight year old pug, leapt onto the bench (quite happily) and stretched the entirety of his body across the letters.

"Elsie has *really* come across quite a puzzle!" exclaimed

Frances as Hubert belly-crawled toward her. Using his nose to push aside the long gold necklace that draped gently over her white, sleeveless blouse, he rested his small head atop her shorts. Frances rubbed generously behind his ears.

It had only been in the last few months that Frances had gradually come to feel comfortable wearing shorts again, and now she wore them unashamedly, accepting the scar that stretched across the front of her leg, and the shorter scar that stretched atop her opposite thigh; they were quite dissimilar in color from the natural soft, brown tones of her skin.

"Where to begin…" Frances murmured, tugging another one of Elsie's letters out from under Hubert's portly belly and considering it thoughtfully.

"The killer?" inquired Bernadine, still inching the walker past the tower of books.

"No." Frances shook her head. "Haven't found the man yet." She tilted her head forward. "Or *woman*," she added, lifting one brow.

"So right, Ms. Franny," Bernadine declared, taking a breath as she finally managed to reach open space. "We women won't tolerate sexism—not one bit. Women can very well be bludgeoners too!"

"Hear, hear, Bernie!"

Bernadine dropped her head as the stack of books she had so carefully avoided suddenly clattered to the floor; for all her painstaking efforts, she had not taken into account her ample hips, which ultimately delivered the inadvertent yet powerful blow. However, Frances hadn't noticed, as she was enthralled with the second page of Elsie's most recent letter.

"And *who* is this James Rennick fellow Elsie seems

so interested in?" she exclaimed, turning over the page. "Apparently he's a guest at the hotel and he looks as handsome as a beagle!"

Hubert snorted in timely fashion, rolling to his other side. Frances eagerly started scribbling a letter in reply. Bernadine positioned the walker in front of her employer.

"And what of the others?" questioned Bernadine, her hands upon her hips.

"What others, Bernie?" asked Frances, lifting her head.

"*Others* should be at the hotel, but Ms. Elsie hasn't said so."

"What *do* you mean, Bernie? Besides the *guests*?"

"Right." Bernie scratched at her head, her auburn hair beginning its descent, today, towards her right side. "I mean is the *owner* of the hotel there? *Shouldn't* he be?"

"My goodness, Bernie! You are an absolute sleuth! It takes a bit of prodding to get it out of you, but you've got it!"

Bernadine nodded toward the walker. "Ready to get started?"

"Not just yet. Do me a favor, will you?" Frances reached for her cordless phone and dialed a number. She then handed the phone to Bernadine. "I'm sure the owner's name is in public records and my realtor will find it faster than anyone... and while you do that I can finish my letter to El." She flashed a smile.

"Ok," agreed Bernadine, taking the phone. "But we've got to get started with your exercises. I'm an honest woman and I'm not paid to lollygag about the place, Ms. Franny."

Bernadine began looking around the room.

"And where did I put my log book?" she mumbled, the phone to her ear. "I've got to make a note of your progress..."

"Good! Go find it, Bernie! I just need to finish this letter."

Frances affectionately gestured Bernadine in the general direction of the door.

"We start *right* when I get back, Ms. Franny!" called Bernadine from over her shoulder. "Oh, it's his answering machine," she mumbled. "Yes," started Bernadine into the phone. "My name is Bernadine Eppler, I'm calling for Ms. Frances Maitland..." Bernadine's voice trailed away as she exited the room.

The hands on Frances's watch journeyed from a quarter past to half past one. The phone rang just as she signed her name at the bottom of the letter.

"Will you answer that for me, Bernie?" she called.

Stuffing the letter into its envelope, Frances looked up to find Bernadine crossing the room.

"It was that gentleman," said Bernadine.

Frances sighed. "If we could just be more specific, Bernie?"

"The realtor," she clarified, holding up a notepad with a name scribbled across the top.

"*That's* the owner of the hotel?" she exclaimed, drawing the pad closer.

"There is no mistake, Ms. Franny. When I heard the name I asked twice just to be sure."

"Well, this is a twist, isn't it?" murmured Frances, resting her fingers to her lips.

With the atmosphere at the hotel being more tense and with there being more questions than answers, Elsie felt compelled to see what she could learn from Paul Hulling. She found him at the hotel's bar, and watched as he helped himself by tilting a crystal decanter, pouring a smooth golden liquid into his glass. Paul was a slender man with dark, closely cropped hair and a slightly crooked nose. His smile was cordial enough, but Elsie wondered what was really on his mind.

"It's a bit early for dinner," he remarked, attributing his behavior to the absence of a bartender. Elsie slid onto the bar stool beside him and took in the stillness of the large, empty dining room. Paul slid her the drink he had just poured. "We've got to help ourselves," he said.

Elsie took a sip, pinching her lips as she swallowed.

"Strong," she choked, setting down the glass.

Paul grinned. "Not much of a drinker?"

Elsie shook her head. "No—*very* little as a matter of fact." She peered at Paul from the side of her eye.

"So," she started, clearing her throat. "What is it that you do, Mr. Hulling? What is your profession?"

He seemed indifferent. "I'm an accountant. I can't say that it's an especially exciting career—for me, at least." He exhaled. "You know, I don't even care for numbers, but it was a practical choice at the time."

"Yes," agreed Elsie, her tone a bit melancholy. "I've often chosen the practical path myself."

Elsie realized that Paul was suddenly studying her for the first time.

"Something is troubling you," he said, resting his glass on the counter top. "I'm not the best company right now, but you can share if you'd like." His shoulders suddenly tensed. "Or has something else happened?"

Resting her elbows against the counter, Elsie massaged gently at her temples.

"James was just taken in for questioning," she said.

"Mr. Rennick?" replied Paul with genuine surprise.

"Apparently he knew the reverend." She looked at Paul thoughtfully. "Possibly even arranged to meet him here."

Paul's brows rose just slightly.

"I see…" he remarked softly.

He took a slow sip. A moment of silence passed between them.

"You sound disappointed," he said finally.

She shrugged. "Yeah, well, I don't really see why I should be." She drew in a breath and spun her stool to face Paul. "Enough about all that. What about you, Mr. Hulling? How did you manage to get stuck here?"

"I've been asking myself that same question since I got here."

"You didn't get an invitation like the others?" asked Elsie.

"The opposite, in fact."

He dropped his head into the palms of his hands. Elsie reached behind the bar for a bottle of water.

"I'm afraid the alcohol may be getting to you, Mr. Hulling. You're starting to slur just a little bit." She placed the water in front of him.

"I've found something out," he said, taking a deep breath.

Elsie stilled, silently mouthing Paul's words.

"Say that again," she said aloud.

"Why I'm here," he clarified. "It's because I've found something out."

Elsie suddenly recalled the strange conversation between the man and woman just outside her bedroom door.

It was Paul Hulling, she realized. *He was the man outside her door… But who was the woman?*

James Rennick was at that moment being questioned by Sergeant Wilcox at the police station.

"Mr. Rennick, this doesn't look good."

The sergeant slapped the small address book onto his desk as Officer Jenkins leaned against his own. James had been guided across the scuffed linoleum floor and offered a seat in front of Sergeant Wilcox. Crossing his arms, the sergeant said nothing, unnerving James.

"No," said the sergeant finally, shaking his head. "This doesn't look good at all. It would seem, Mr. Rennick, that you knew one of our victims, but you kept this information to yourself."

James ran his fingers through his hair and scooted his chair closer. "Yes," he stated plainly. "But it's not because I *did* anything."

His heel tapped steadily against the floor as he explained.

"I didn't say anything because I didn't want... Well, because I didn't want *this* to happen."

"Being caught for murder, you mean?"

"No!" James's eyes darted between Officer Jenkins and the sergeant. "You have to believe me. It's all a misunderstanding," he pleaded. "I mean, I *did* know Reverend Pennington, just not well, and I certainly didn't kill him."

The sergeant waited. James swallowed and continued.

"It was something I saw in the paper, about the Wellings. It was the day after I had arrived at the hotel that I saw a headline about them—that they had gotten married."

Sergeant Wilcox listened carefully, casting only a brief glance at his officer.

"As you know, I'm a journalist. I tend to notice things, possible stories I could write about."

"Go on," said Officer Jenkins. "What did you notice about the Wellings?"

"In the *Tribune*", James explained, "there was a huge photo of the couple and I noticed that Olivia Welling looked a lot like a woman I briefly met in Dansford."

"So?" asked the sergeant. "What does this have to do with the reverend?"

"Well, that's just it," said James. "It was when I was doing a story on Reverend Pennington." He debated. "I think it was at some charity event I was covering a few years ago. The point is that it was *there*, in the town of Dansford, that I noticed her—the same woman that I think is Olivia Welling. She had just gotten *married* and it was Reverend Pennington who officiated the ceremony…"

A brief moment passed before Sergeant Wilcox's eyes widened in comprehension.

"You're telling me Mrs. Welling is already married?"

"Well, that's the problem," said James, "I'm not sure. There are a few possibilities. If she *is* the woman I think she is then she might already be married. Of course, I couldn't just look her up. Her name certainly wasn't Olivia Welling back then. So, you see, that's why I needed the reverend to come to the hotel. I wasn't certain, and I needed to be if I was going to crack this scandal wide open. Millionaire marries woman with no pre-nup only to find out that she's already married! It would have been *huge*. Readers eat these type of stories up."

"Even if she was married, she might have gotten a divorce," suggested Officer Jenkins.

James nodded adamantly. "I agree. In fact, I wondered

much about that myself, but then, while a few of us were conversing by the hotel's tennis court, her husband remarked to his wife that she only has one honeymoon in life and she should be enjoying it. That sounds like a man who believed his wife was never married. Of course, I still needed to confirm that Olivia Welling was the same woman I saw get married in Dansford. So I was stuck. I had to wait for the reverend to identify her for me before I could say anything about what I suspected."

"So what did you do?" asked Sergeant Wilcox.

"I called the reverend. I told him I needed his help, and I knew he would want to clear things up because he is a righteous man. He takes the covenant of marriage very seriously."

"And you thought he'd be all right with you splashing it about in the headlines?" asked Officer Jenkins.

Embarrassed, James remarked: "Ok, no. I didn't mention any of *that* to him, but if my theory was correct, I still think Mr. Welling would deserve to know."

"And did the reverend confirm that Olivia Welling was already married?"

"No. He was murdered before he had a chance."

Elsie and Paul were still seated at the hotel's bar, but she found herself somewhat frustrated in that she had made very little progress in uncovering what he knew. She definitely couldn't miss this opportunity, yet Paul's inebriated state continued to make things more difficult. She persisted:

"Mr. Hulling, what have you found out?"

Paul didn't reply. He stared blankly ahead, the empty glass resting comfortably in his grip.

"Mr. Hulling?" she pressed. "What have you discovered?"

"Mothers."

Elsie's head fell gently to one side.

"*Mothers?*" she asked.

Paul nodded. "They always know what's best, don't they? They always want you to settle down and live a happy life. They make life seem so easy when you're young."

Elsie opened her mouth to reply but hesitated.

Mothers, thought Elsie. *To find the McCray child from twenty years ago could be the key to it all.* She shook herself free of Franny's voice, which was playing in the forefront of her mind. She focused intently on Paul.

"It's not always easy, though," he went on. "I've never been especially courageous. You don't want to risk losing things, even the little you have, but mothers—now *they* will always believe in you."

He slid his empty glass to the side.

"And… your dad?" asked Elsie, "What was he like?"

Paul shook his head. "He died when I was young. I can't say that I really knew him."

"I'm sorry."

Silence lingered for a while.

"I've got to be courageous now, though, don't I?" he said, dragging the palms of his hands across his face. "I've got to get this business over with."

"What are you talking about, Mr. Hulling?"

The hotel's sturdy front door slammed against the wall, the noise echoing throughout the lobby. Paul spun around on his stool and stumbled as he slid from his seat. Elsie caught his arm and helped him to regain his footing.

"Something's happened?" asked Paul as he seemed to be awakened by the loud sound.

Just then, Sergeant Wilcox's voice boomed through the lobby.

"Mr. Needling?"

The sergeant's meaty hand struck the small, gold service bell mercilessly.

"Sergeant Wilcox?" remarked Mr. Turnbull, rising from his seat by the fire. He looked keenly between the sergeant and the officer. "What's happened?" he asked. "Where is James?"

"Still at the police station, Mr. Turnbull. I have not finished my inquiries." The sergeant looked crossly in his direction. "I've got an investigation to conduct," he added, striking the service bell once more. "Allow me to conduct it."

Elsie and Paul stepped into the lobby. Paul was attempting to shake his head free from the effects of the alcohol.

Mr. Turnbull cursed under his breath as Mrs. Tidwell jerked awake from her inadvertent slumber in the chair next to his. Confusion swept across her face as she tried to recall just where she had fallen asleep. She touched her arm and leg curiously, her eyes widening as she caught sight of Mr. Turnbull.

"The *hotel*," she murmured excitedly in remembrance.

She peered toward Mr. Needling who had charged into the lobby from his office.

"*What* is all this about?" demanded the manager, slowing his steps when he caught sight of the sergeant. Straightening his jacket, Mr. Needling cleared his throat. "Has something happened, Sergeant?" he inquired in a milder tone.

"There's been a *development*," chimed Mrs. Tidwell, breathlessly.

"Where is Mrs. Olivia Welling?" questioned the sergeant. "I need to speak with her immediately."

Mr. Needling's head drew back. "Mrs. Welling... Yes, of course. I expect she is in her room." He patted his pockets helplessly. "A key? You would need a key, perhaps? Or... don't you?"

"Nonsense!" exclaimed Mr. Turnbull. "He's the sergeant. He can go where he pleases!"

"Not without a warrant. We do have *laws*," countered Paul, stepping forward.

"Still, I'd say he probably should have a key," decided Mrs. Tidwell.

Sergeant Wilcox pinched the bridge of his nose.

"But the question is," continued Mr. Needling, "would you rather... knock, Sergeant?" He leaned forward. "Or is this a—a more," he lowered his voice, "a more *forceful* type of situation? Guns blazing sort of thing?"

"*Ooooh,* how *thrilling*," purred Mrs. Tidwell.

"*Mr. Needling*!" barked the sergeant. "Just take me to her room."

"Oh!" Mr. Needling rushed out from behind the counter. "Of course. This way, *please*."

Mr. Needling had only taken a few steps when Dr. Linder suddenly rushed in through the open doors of the hotel. Almost immediately he settled his eyes on the imposing build of Sergeant Wilcox.

"Sergeant!" called the doctor.

"Not now, Doc!" yelled the sergeant from over his shoulder. "I've got business to handle."

"But *Sergeant!*"

"What did I just say, Doctor?!" growled Sergeant Wilcox, turning.

"I was here the night of the murder," hissed Dr. Linder with surprising asperity.

"I *know* this, Doctor. What's your point?"

"I was *here* because I had to see a patient staying at the hotel—one of *your* interested parties, Sergeant."

The sergeant lifted his chin and waited.

"I sent a blood sample to the lab", continued Dr. Linder, "and I only just received the results."

He lifted a sheet of paper, its edges crinkling under the stern grip of his fingers.

"What's that got to do with—"

"It's Marian Hartwell," interjected the doctor. "She is being poisoned."

Chapter 9
MARIAN HARTWELL

OLIVIA WELLING'S EYES fluttered open as a succession of footsteps and frantic chatter in the hallway woke her from her afternoon nap.

Mr. Welling emerged from the bathroom.

"What's all that commotion in the hallway?" he questioned, tossing his hand towel across the chair.

A booming voice from the hall yelled: "Marian! *Open the door.*"

"I'm not sure," replied Olivia, throwing off her covers. "Something's definitely wrong."

She reached for the shawl that was draped across the foot of her bed and quietly pulled her door open. Crowded outside Marian Hartwell's room were Sergeant Wilcox, Dr. Linder, Mr. Needling and a slew of the other guests.

"Just give me the key," demanded Sergeant Wilcox.

Olivia stepped into the hall. "What's going on?" she asked.

"There, I'm in," said the sergeant, handing back the key to

Mr. Needling. "Marian," he called, his voice distant as he cautiously entered the room. Dr. Linder followed closely behind.

"No," instructed Dr. Linder, pressing his palm against Paul's chest. "Everyone please give us space. No one should enter."

Mrs. Tidwell objected to this mandate. Olivia marched toward Mr. Needling, her husband looking on curiously as he rested his shoulder against the frame of his door.

"Mr. Needling, I demand to know what's going on," reiterated Olivia.

Iradene Hartwell noiselessly maneuvered between the other guests, forcing her way into the room and staring silently at her sister.

"I can barely feel a pulse," stated Dr. Linder. "Come, help me prop her up."

Olivia shivered as the sergeant rested Marian against the headboard, her pale face falling forward.

"What—what's happened to her?" asked Olivia, wrapping her burgundy shawl more tightly around her shoulders. Mr. Welling approached his wife and she fell into his chest.

"Apparently she was poisoned," murmured Elsie.

Mr. Needling pushed through the group.

"Please move out the way! There has got to be a clear path! Please *make way!*" he demanded. He turned toward the sergeant. "The ambulance is downstairs. Shall I have them bring up the stretcher?"

The sergeant shook his head.

"It would take too long with those stairs. Let's just carry her. Dr. Linder, help move the covers for me and I'll lift—"

"Give her to me," demanded Paul, striding into the room. "I'll carry her."

Both the sergeant and the doctor turned sharply toward Paul.

"*I* will carry her," he insisted.

Sergeant Wilcox nodded, stepping aside. "But hurry," he growled.

Paul gently lifted Marian and her head rolled into his shoulder.

"It's all right, Mar," he whispered, his chin grazing the top of her head. "It's all right, baby."

Iradene's jaw fell slack as Paul hurriedly carried her sister down the long corridor. Dr. Linder and Sergeant Wilcox rushed behind Marian's limp, frail body as an uneasy silence fell over the rest of the group—except, of course, for Mrs. Tidwell.

"'*Baby!*'" she exclaimed, tipping her head forward. Peering over the rim of her glasses, Mrs. Tidwell's eyes followed Paul and Marian as they descended the stairs. "Are they…? Is *he*…?"

She slid her glasses back into place as Paul and Marian faded from her line of sight.

"Mmm *hmmm…*" she hummed with great satisfaction.

⸎ ⸎

Several hours had passed since Marian had been taken to the hospital. No word had arrived of her condition, but much speculation had swirled among the other guests. Fatigue, however, had eventually settled upon the group, much to Mrs. Tidwell's dismay, and all had retired to their rooms. Elsie remained awake in her bed, attempting to sort through all of her thoughts. Flicking on her light, she addressed another letter to her sister.

Dear Franny, I'll just cut to the chase.

Her handwriting was less careful than usual as she scribbled her thoughts hurriedly across the page.

It was Paul Hulling I heard whispering outside my room a few nights ago—and I'm now almost certain it was Marian to whom he was whispering! What's interesting is that Paul wanted, but was unable, to tell Marian something important that night. The question is what? What did he know? Did he ever get a chance to tell her? After having spoken to Paul earlier today, I strongly suspect that he didn't. I don't think he could gather enough courage to say whatever it was he needed to say. They've clearly got a secret relationship and, based on the way Ms. Iradene Hartwell looked at him tonight, I suspect she is the reason they kept it under wraps. She looked displeased, to say the least.

What's worse, though, is that someone has been poisoning Marian! Like the poor creature isn't broken enough! Franny, I'm no doctor, but I can tell you that she was near death when they took her out of that room. Someone wanted her out the way! But why? Was it something she knew about the murders? Something she saw that someone feared she would talk about? I wouldn't be surprised if that was the case as Marian seems scared to even speak socially, let alone if she were witness to a crime here in the hotel!

That brings me to the initial murders. The murders—

Elsie hesitated for a moment and started again.

Norma Kemper's murder and Reverend Pennington's murder seem…

wrong. I know, I know—morally wrong obviously, but what I mean is that the methods used to kill them were so different. Norma's murder and Marian's attempted murder were both done using poison, while the reverend's was done with a blunt instrument. It just seems like we've gone from one extreme to the next, as far as killing goes (if there is such a thing).

She considered for a moment.

But then why bash anyone over the head at all if you've got poison? And even then, why kill Norma and Marian so slowly? Norma was being poisoned for three days by an herb: white snakeroot. Now that I think of it, Marian always looked pretty ill whenever I saw her at dinner, so I suspect she was being poisoned that entire time. Poison can be a quick sort of business if one wants it to be, so why drag it out?

Oh! And there's something else. What if I told you that Paul Hulling was only raised by his mother—no father? He is of the right age and his father died when he was young. Could he be the child from twenty years ago?

Elsie pressed her pen against the paper, but this time she was thoughtful with each word.

I'm a little saddened to report that James has been taken in for questioning. Apparently he knew the reverend and even invited him here to the hotel! It makes me wonder what else he hasn't told me—not that he is required to tell me anything, of course, but his having invited the reverend here ought to have been mentioned, don't you think?

I don't want to believe it, but I can't ignore the possibility that James could be guilty or involved somehow. And do you remember that thing that's been nagging at me? That's been sitting in the back of my mind but that I couldn't recall? I remember it now. It was only after I started seriously considering James as a suspect that it came to me...

He's got a scar, Fran. James has got a scar just above his right eye. And the child from twenty years ago fell on the rocks out by the cliffs, obtaining an injury just above the right eye. So who is it? James? Paul? Olivia? Remember, she grew up without a father.

Speaking of Olivia, the sergeant came here tonight determined to speak to her about something. I wonder what he's uncovered on her.

What weighs most heavily on me, though, is motive. Why was anyone murdered? And look at Marian. I keep trying to figure that out. Who would want to hurt her?

Marian and Paul... Marian and Paul... I think of them as a pair now, and the way he spoke to her tonight...

Elsie shook her head.

I would rule him out of the lineup based only on a small hunch: I can't imagine him hurting Marian now that I know they are a couple.

She dropped her pen.

"I need to search Paul's room," she said suddenly.

Leaping from her bed, she reached for her robe.

"He didn't want to just *tell* her something," she murmured excitedly, recalling the couple's clandestine conversation they held just outside her door. "He said he wanted to *show* her something."

She looked at the clock. It was past midnight.

"No," she said decidedly, digging into her purse, "He probably hasn't come back to the hotel yet."

Elsie retrieved a small flashlight from her bag and rushed across the room. Cracking open the door, she peered down the empty, dimly lit hall. Everyone had gone to bed. *Good.* She crept down the hall and onto the main stairway, tiptoed toward the front desk and cast a hurried glance toward the fireplace to make sure that Mr. Turnbull hadn't fallen asleep in his favorite chair. The excitement, decided Elsie, was probably too much for him; he had indeed gone to bed. Slinking behind the receptionist desk, she swept a finger across a case of small mahogany cubbies in which the hotel's room keys dangled. She gripped Paul's room number and moved swiftly back the way she had come.

Drawing in a deep breath, Elsie stepped up to Paul's door and pressed her ear to the wood. She heard nothing so she proceeded to unlock the door and enter the dark room.

"Umph."

Paul's room, apparently, was not arranged like her own. Rubbing her knee, she clicked on her flashlight and steadied the vase that had danced dangerously close to the edge of the writing desk. Slowly she pointed her light across the room.

"If I wanted to hide something", considered Elsie aloud as she stepped gingerly through the darkness, "I would conceal it in a part of the room where visitors wouldn't stumble across it." She walked past the bed and pulled open a double set of doors. "Perhaps the armoire…"

She slid aside a handful of shirts that were hanging above a single piece of luggage. The suitcase was already partially open, so she knelt beside it and gently sorted through the clothes inside.

"Nothing," she mumbled faintly, the small flashlight gripped between her teeth. Replacing the bag, she stood and cast her eye from one part of the room to the next.

"*Of course.*"

A small smile tugged at the corners of her lips.

She entered the bathroom and peered hurriedly through the cabinets.

"Not here," she muttered quietly.

Turning, her eyes fell on the large mirror which rested, unattached, atop the vanity. She slid her hand across the backing, her fingers rising as they stumbled against something flat that was anchored behind the mirror. She tugged and tore it free from its taped edges. An excited rush came over her as she studied the large manila envelope. It was addressed to Mr. Paul Hulling.

"From a Jonathan Davis," read Elsie aloud as she pulled a set of documents from the envelope. Stamped at the top, in bright red ink, was the word "COPY". Skimming the text, Elsie gasped.

⁂

Only a few doors down from Paul's room another guest was lying awake, restless. She turned her head; she was certain she had heard Paul return to his room.

Climbing from her bed, she wrapped herself in a burgundy shawl and pulled it over her head. No one was in the hall. *Good.* Slowly she crept toward Mr. Hulling's door.

So Marian and Paul were secretly seeing each other. If I had only known!

She stifled a snort. Things had not gone to plan, and now *this*. She turned to face the door.

Yes, something has to be done.

She turned the knob and stepped into the dark room. A dim light radiated from the bathroom. *He must be in there.* Gripping the vase beside the door, she approached the bathroom; she turned the base of the vase upward in her hand and crept closer, lifting her arm.

❧ ❧

Elsie's fingers brushed gingerly over the photocopied document. Still only halfway through the text she shook her head, overwhelmed by what she had discovered.

"I also leave," she continued aloud, "to my youngest daughter, Marian Hartwell, the total sum of half of my entire estate, totaling 34 million dollars, to be held in trust until she has either reached the age of thirty-five or married."

Elsie whistled.

"Marian is in line to receive *34 million*," she uttered, returning her eyes to the paper and moving them swiftly down the page. "Some more legal mumbo jumbo," she muttered, finally reaching the end. As she lifted the bottom corner of the page, her hand stilled.

"*Oh…*"

She drew the paper closer, straining to make out the signature.

Yes, it's a bit sloppy, she thought, *but it is definitely his.*

She lifted her head.

"This document was *witnessed* by Reverend Pennington…"

Turning excitedly on her heel, she shrieked as a shadowed figure plunged the base of a vase toward her head.

Chapter 10
ELSIE'S NOT CONVINCED

PAIN SHOT THROUGH Elsie's arm as she lifted it just in time to take the brunt of the blow. The shadowed figure lifted the vase once more, but Elsie dipped her shoulder and lunged forward into the intruder's chest, inciting a piercing cry through the darkness. Excited voices began to echo down the hall, drawing nearer as the vase crashed to the floor and the sound resonated throughout the room.

Gripping her throbbing arm, Elsie rushed toward the front of the room.

"In here!" she yelled, stumbling back as the door swung open.

Her eyes struggled to adjust to the hallway lights that streamed into the darkness. Mr. Turnbull staggered into the room first, with Mr. Welling, Mrs. Tidwell and Mr. Needling following closely behind.

"Ms. Maitland!" exclaimed Mr. Turnbull.

"Someone attacked me!" yelled Elsie, wincing as she

lifted her arm to direct them. "The bathroom—check the bathroom."

Mr. Welling strode forcefully past Mr. Turnbull toward the body slumped just outside the bathroom door.

"Isn't that your wife's burgundy shawl?" asked Mrs. Tidwell, slowly approaching the body. She tottered back as Mr. Welling turned sharply toward her.

"I hope you're not implying what I think you are," he growled.

"N—no, I only meant…"

Mrs. Tidwell gasped as Olivia Welling entered the room.

"But your shawl," uttered Mrs. Tidwell, pointing to the burgundy fabric that covered the intruder's upper body and face.

Olivia peered over her husband's shoulder toward the body.

"That's my shawl, all right," she readily admitted. "I accidently left it downstairs and only realized after I had gone to bed. I planned to get it in the morning, but it looks like someone else beat me to it." Olivia nodded toward the floor. "Who is it?" she asked.

"Oh my," muttered Mr. Needling. "Oh my. The sergeant isn't here yet. Shouldn't we wait to touch the body?"

"Wait for what?" exclaimed Elsie.

"The intruder isn't *dead*," stated Mr. Turnbull. "Look, there's some movement."

"Just pick up the shawl," demanded Olivia.

Mr. Welling nodded. Stooping beside the body, he slid the soft fabric toward him.

"Huh!" exclaimed Mr. Turnbull. "I told you that woman was no good."

"*Iradene Hartwell?*" asked Mrs. Tidwell. "But why—why come to your room, Ms. Maitland? Why attack you?"

Heat rose in Elsie's cheeks.

"This isn't actually *my* room," she murmured.

"It certainly isn't," stated Mr. Needling, pulling his shoulders back. "It's Mr. Paul Hulling's."

Mr. Turnbull grunted. "I think you ought to explain, my girl," he said, lifting his hefty head upward. "Yes, you ought to explain."

❦

Sergeant Wilcox took a seat at the hotel's long, wooden kitchen table. Casting an irritated glance at Elsie, he brushed his hands over his head and asked:

"Do you know what time it is, Ms. Maitland?"

Mr. Needling handed the sergeant a cup of coffee. "Thanks," he grumbled, lifting the mug toward his nose.

Elsie was slow to respond. "Just after 3 am…"

"Correct."

The sergeant took a generous sip of his coffee. Finally he set the mug on the table and continued. "So that means, Ms. Maitland, that you must have begun your little adventure to Paul Hulling's room sometime before that, while others were asleep… because you didn't want anyone to know what you were up to."

"Not exactly," said Elsie, rubbing gingerly at her bandaged arm. "I wasn't doing anything wrong."

The sergeant looked at her doubtfully.

"I mean, not *wrong* like you're thinking," she added. "I had a hunch, is all. I thought that Mr. Hulling was hiding some-thing—and I was right. And it's *critical* to your case."

The sergeant's forehead creased, but he made no reply and allowed Elsie to continue.

"But when I turned to leave, that—that *crazy* woman, Iradene Hartwell, tried to kill me with a vase!"

Leaning forward, the sergeant rested his elbows against the table. "So then, what I need to know, Ms. Maitland, is what you have uncovered."

Elsie slid the envelope across the table.

"We know", she explained, "that Marian Hartwell and Paul Hulling have a relationship, right?"

"Perhaps," replied the sergeant noncommittally.

"Ok, fine. Let's just assume for a moment that state-ment is true and Paul and Marian are in a relationship, even a potentially serious relationship, but that they've had to keep it a secret from her mentally abusive older sister, Iradene. You don't have to be a rocket scientist to see that Iradene keeps Marian on a tight leash."

Sergeant Wilcox pulled the copied documents from the envelope.

"Paul had these papers *hidden* in his room, which means they were of value to someone else. If you look here", she pointed, "it states that *Marian* was set to inherit a massive sum of money once she turned thirty-five—which I imagine will be soon—*or* once she gets married."

"Perhaps to Mr. Hulling," murmured Sergeant Wilcox.

"*Exactly.*" Elsie leaned forward. "But that's not it."

The sergeant lifted his eyes.

"Let's say that Marian doesn't *know* she is meant to inherit this money. My brief observations give me the impression that

Marian believes she will forever be under her sister's tyranny. If you knew you were going to inherit *34 million* dollars you'd more likely adopt an attitude that says, 'I've got options, a future ahead of me', right?"

The sergeant showed some approval as he read through the document, silently assessing all that Elsie had said.

"I think that Paul Hulling," continued Elsie, "found this out and came to rescue his maiden. This was clearly difficult for him, though, because Marian was obviously reluctant to leave her sister, as many in abusive relationships are."

The sergeant agreed.

"Your suggestion seems quite plausible," he decided aloud.

"But if Paul Hulling could show her *this*", said Elsie, pointing to the page, "then perhaps he could persuade her to leave. The only problem is I don't think he ever did—not before she was poisoned, I mean."

The sergeant beckoned Mr. Needling for more coffee and started: "So Iradene Hartwell saw you enter Mr. Hulling's room. She followed you in and tried to kill you because you uncovered this information?"

Elsie hesitated.

"I'm not sure…" she said.

Sergeant Wilcox waited.

"She might have thought I was Paul," suggested Elsie. "The room was too dark to see much of anything. She probably made out my figure with the beam from my flashlight, but I can't imagine she saw much else."

The sergeant rubbed gingerly at his eyes.

"This is like a house of horrors," he mumbled. I've got *two* murders and *two* attempted murders and it's not even daybreak."

"No, but half your battle is won," countered Elsie, her voice rising as she considered another possibility aloud. "Iradene Hartwell's plan was *always* to get rid of her sister before she could inherit. I mean, she'd have to, right? If she didn't want her sister to get the money?"

"What are you suggesting, Ms. Maitland? That Iradene Hartwell came here to kill her sister?"

"No, not exactly. I think Iradene Hartwell really did come here because she received a letter, just like the rest of the guests from twenty years ago, but I think Iradene was *already* poisoning her sister. I remember the first night at dinner Marian didn't look well at all."

The sergeant reflected. "Really, this trip probably saved her. Had Dr. Linder not gotten to her in time, Marian would probably have died."

"Right, so Iradene saw that Marian would now survive, and ultimately be able to claim her inheritance at the stipulated age of thirty-five. Iradene's fear, of course, is that she would no longer have access to that money. To make matters worse, we all heard Paul call Marian 'baby'," pronounced Elsie.

"Why is that important?" asked the sergeant.

"When Paul referred to Marian as 'baby' Iradene realized that Paul Hulling was clearly on intimate terms with her. Therefore, if Marian married Paul, she would automatically receive her full inheritance also stipulated by the will. Again, putting Iradene at risk for losing access to Marian's money."

"Iradene Hartwell", stated the sergeant, "is responsible for the attempted murders of her sister, Marian, and you—although that was intended for Paul Hulling."

"That's right," agreed Elsie. "Oh, and she also murdered Reverend Pennington."

Sergeant Wilcox flinched as a glass shattered across the kitchen floor. Mr. Needling, who had been silently sitting in the corner of the room, stood and rushed toward them excitedly.

"You've solved it then!?" he gushed, his thinning, uncombed hair standing wild yet proud atop his head. "This whole terrible mess is over?"

"Mr. Needling," replied the sergeant. "I've said no such thing."

"B—but…"

"We are still working out the details, Mr. Needling."

The hotel manager slumped into a chair beside Elsie. "My business will be *ruined* if this isn't resolved. Do you know I've already had *eight* cancellations? And *they* were just after the first two murders! Now when the papers get wind of *this*…!"

He shot up from his chair.

"Please come to the Hotel Westend," he murmured, pacing the kitchen floor and flailing his arms above his head. "You can get bludgeoned on the head or poisoned or maybe even suffer a concussion."

Sergeant Wilcox returned his attention to Elsie.

"Right, so Iradene Hartwell murdered the reverend, you say?"

Elsie stretched her arm across the table, wincing as it bumped the table's edge. "Take a look at this signature," she said, tapping the page.

The sergeant looked over the name.

"A bit hard to read," he remarked, studying it closely. "Is that Richard…?" He tilted his head to the side. "Ah!"

Elsie grinned.

"Reverend…"

He lifted his head, stunned.

"Reverend Henry Pennington?!"

"It looks like Paul wasn't the only one who knew Marian stood to inherit," said Elsie. "Reverend Pennington knew and, unfortunately for him, he was staying at the same hotel as Iradene Hartwell."

"My guess", added the sergeant, "is that Iradene Hartwell figured it was only a matter of time before the reverend struck up a conversation with Marian, and Iradene couldn't take a chance that he would remark on her inheritance, especially since she was coming up on the specified age."

"So she killed him," remarked Elsie sadly. "While everyone was running downstairs looking for the crying baby, she took a chance."

Sergeant Wilcox stood. "It wouldn't have taken long. His door was open. Everyone was distracted, rushing in the opposite direction. Poor guy certainly wouldn't have expected it. Probably had his back turned. He was frail, she came up behind him with the lamp, the same way she tried to do with you—"

"Yeah, but I could fight back."

The sergeant brushed his hand across the stubble on his chin.

"Mr. Needling," he called, turning to find the hotel manager seated at the end of the long kitchen table, his face planted nose down against the wood counter and his arms sprawled out beside him. "You can stop banging your head against the table. We've got the murderer in custody."

"Normally that's just a figure of speech," whispered Elsie.

The sergeant shared a smile with her. Mr. Needling lifted

his head, his small eyes blinking away the daze set upon him by exhaustion.

"It's over?" he asked hesitantly.

"That's right, Mr. Needling," replied the sergeant. "I've got ample evidence here," he added, lifting the documents.

Mr. Needling slid back into his chair—relieved, but tired. "Maybe now I can finally hire a maid," he murmured, slicking back his hair only for it to spring back to attention. "No maid has wanted to work here after what happened to Norma."

"Well, I'm sure that won't be a problem now," said the sergeant, moving toward the doorway.

"I advertised incentives: wage increases, extra vacation days! *Still* no applicants!" Mr. Needling's face fell. "Except, of course, for Mr. Johansson's child. *Completely* incompetent."

The sergeant looked in Elsie's direction. "Ms. Maitland," he acknowledged, before leaving the room.

"If I had hired that young woman to be my maid, she would have ruined my business in two weeks tops!" Mr. Needling went on.

"The maid," murmured Elsie. She jumped up from her chair and rushed into the hall after the sergeant, who was crossing through the lobby. "Sergeant Wilcox!" she called. "Sergeant Wilcox! What about *Norma*?"

He turned, frowning. "Norma? What about her?"

"*Why* did Iradene kill the maid? That's still not entirely clear. It doesn't make any sense."

"Don't you worry about that, Ms. Maitland," he said, pulling open the hotel's front doors. "I'll coax the information out of Ms. Hartwell yet."

He turned and drew the hotel's doors closed behind him.

"I don't think it's over," remarked a man, his voice deep and weary.

Elsie spun around as Mr. Turnbull stirred from his favorite chair by the fireplace.

"No, this whole business isn't over," he reiterated softly.

"I almost didn't see you there, Mr. Turnbull," remarked Elsie breathlessly. "I guess I'm still a little shaken."

Mr. Turnbull stood and tightened the belt of his robe. He gave a small nod. "Goodnight, Ms. Maitland."

Elsie stood alone in the hotel's lobby, watching as Mr. Turnbull climbed the stairs. She listened as he gently closed the door to his bedroom, the crisp clang of his lock echoing throughout the hotel.

⁊ ⸎

Mr. Tidwell arrived at the Hotel Westend at precisely eight in the morning. Slapping the *Gazette*'s morning edition onto the reception desk, he came straight to the point.

"I've come to collect my wife."

Mr. Needling looked down at the newspaper headline.

ANOTHER ATTEMPT AT HOTEL HOMICIDE

Beads of sweat formed on his forehead.

"I can assure you, sir," began Mr. Needling, clearing his throat, "your wife and the rest of our guests are perfectly safe now. I'm sure the paper has also reported that an arrest has been made."

"It has," confirmed Mr. Tidwell. "But I've also got it on good word that the sergeant still has that other young man in his custody which tells me that the case is still active."

Mr. Needling wiped a shaky hand across his brow. "That's

just for questioning, I'm sure," he explained. "I expect Mr. Rennick will be back any time now. I really do apologize for any worry this might have caused."

Mr. Tidwell felt a tinge of guilt. "I'm sorry, Dennis, I know you can't help all this, but the fact is that I just don't feel comfortable with my wife staying in a place where—"

"Of course, sir." Mr. Needling collected a key from the wall behind him. "If you'll give me just a moment?"

Mr. Tidwell offered his thanks as Elsie descended the stairs. "Mr. Tidwell, isn't it?"

He extended his hand. "That's right. A pleasure to see you again, Ms.—?"

"Maitland," replied Elsie, smiling. "You have more fish to deliver?"

Mr. Tidwell shook his head. "No, not today. I've actually come for my wife." He paused a moment, looking at Elsie's bandaged arm. "I saw the paper this morning."

Elsie nodded. "I'll just say it wasn't my favorite night."

"Well, I am glad that you're okay. I know the sergeant has arrested Iradene Hartwell, but I still felt that I should come and get Vesta. She never has known when to back out of things—she just wants to gossip, you understand?"

"Mrs. Tidwell does strike me as an extraordinarily inquisitive woman," replied Elsie.

Mr. Tidwell laughed. "How kind of you! I've heard far worse!"

"George! What on earth are you doing here?!"

Mrs. Tidwell hobbled down the stairway, her gray hair slightly matted on one side and her pink cheeks flushed.

"I've come to take you home, Vesta."

"But I've only just gotten here!"

Elsie slid away and sank into one of the wingback chairs by the fireplace.

"Please tell me you at least brought me the paper?"

Mr. Tidwell lifted the *Gazette*, keeping it at arm's length from his wife.

"Now can we go, Vesta? It's ridiculous that you're even staying here at all."

Mrs. Tidwell lunged forward on her good leg and seized the newsprint from her husband's hand in quick, mongoose-like fashion. Mr. Tidwell threw up his arms as she hurriedly scanned the front page.

"That's right, yes, that's about right," she murmured. "Ha!" She lifted her head. "Iradene Hartwell a mastermind criminal *indeed*!"

"Vesta, *dear*," encouraged her husband, guiding her toward the door. "Let's go."

"And what about the *Tribune*?" she demanded, pulling her arm from her husband's.

"The *Tribune*?" he asked.

"I need a copy of *their* report on this," she said, striking her hand against the paper. "My goodness, George, I'm virtually a *suspect* in the investigation!"

"Hardly, dear."

"George, you *always* get me a copy and out of all the times to forget, you forget *now*?!"

"I didn't forget, dear. I simply haven't gone to the station to obtain a copy. I came here first as I felt you were in *danger*."

"How utterly inconsiderate!" she exclaimed, lumbering out of the hotel, an obvious limp in her gait.

A deep breath escaped Mr. Needling as he watched Mr. Tidwell hurry behind his wife.

From her position by the fireplace, Elsie noticed Mr. Needling's expression soften.

"Relieved?" she asked amiably.

His face flushed a deep red. "I—I suppose that came out the wrong way," he stammered. "It's just, well, gossip might make things worse and—"

Elsie grinned. "No need to explain."

Mr. Needling cleared his throat.

"I've got a letter for you, Ms. Maitland—overnighted," he said, handing it to her across the front desk.

Elsie recognized her sister's handwriting. Reclaiming her seat, she tore eagerly through the envelope.

Dear El,

I've got a handful of your letters before me and Bernadine has been trying to help sort through the clues!

Curious, Elsie read on.

I'm telling you, El, you might look at Bernie and think she doesn't know a thing, but then you'd be mistaken! Sure, there are times when you talk to her and her thoughts are a bit vague—can't tell whether she's coming or going—but then all of a sudden she gets there and it's eureka*! She is absolutely necessary to one's deductive thought process. She's our Watson, El!*

But to the point. First, as far as James is concerned, you will have to tell me all about him! I'm sure he is a nice guy if he's caught your eye… although, he is technically still a suspect. Bummer, right? My advice?

Keep him close enough to keep an eye on him until you can find out for sure. Oh, and don't date a murderer.

Mr. Needling lifted his eyes as laughter floated upward from Elsie's chair.

And you're right, El. Trying to determine the identity of our mystery child is a tricky matter, so let's leave that for a moment. Sometimes focusing on a different angle brings to light what we couldn't see before. So let's talk about the murders.

Be careful not to make any incorrect assumptions. Do you remember my book, Three Steps, Four Fall? *I wrote four murders, all in the same general setting, but only two were done by the same person. The other two were completely unrelated! It's the same with Norma and Reverend Pennington. Both murders took place in the same location and even at the same time, so many would assume they were linked—an understandable assumption, of course—but if you've learned anything from my novels, you know there is very rarely ever just one possibility.*

This encouraged Elsie to rethink her approach to solving Norma's death. She read on eagerly:

Take away that link, El. You might very well have two killers (or more, if you want to be technical)! Break down each murder as if it was its own case and see what you get.

Oh, and I almost forgot to tell you. I was reading my Bible last night and I came across that quote the reverend said about justice, the one you like so much. It's actually from Scripture. The book of Amos, chapter 5, verse 24.

Well, I've got to go, El. Bernadine is getting ready to stretch my muscles, or is it 'build them up'? Either way, make them into finely tuned machines! Currently, though, she has gone in search of her log book. You two would get along well, I think. She too has a tendency to misplace things. Not on as grand a scale as you but, still, it is common ground nevertheless.

I tell you, El, I love Bernie, but God forbid if my heart conks out! I'd be dead before she found the paddles!

All right. I hear her coming down the hall. Keep me posted, little sister.

Love you

—Franny

Elsie smiled, thinking of the advice her sister had imparted. Refolding the letter, she noticed a post script on the back of the page:

El, my Watson has returned with some startling new information!

Elsie drew the letter closer.

On Bernie's suggestion, we decided that it wouldn't hurt if we determined the owner of the Hotel Westend—perhaps he or she could provide us some additional clues. Well, Bernadine just heard back from my realtor and we've got a name, El.

The owner of the hotel is a man by the name of Ted Rennick. Yes, Rennick. This man must somehow be related to James, your little beagle boy with droopy eyes. The owner of the hotel and James Rennick must be connected somehow. If not, then this is one huge coincidence.

Elsie fell back into her chair. There was no question now that James was involved in this fiasco, but how? She closed her eyes, running questions over in her mind. *If someone related to James owns the hotel, then why would he have received a prize to come here? Unless there was no prize at all and James came up with that lie so people wouldn't suspect him of being involved.*

Elsie jumped from her seat as the front door to the hotel swung open and banged against the wall. She immediately recognized the bearded man from the cliffs.

"*Excuse* me, sir!" yelled Mr. Needling. "Is there a problem here?!"

"Is it true that Iradene Hartwell has been arrested for the murders?"

"I—I…" Mr. Needling was briefly taken aback, but immediately persevered. For in his mind, he was a decorated manager of a hotel that had survived *two* murders and *two* attempted murders. It was thanks to this self-awareness that he was not going to take any guff from anyone—and certainly not on *this* morning, of all days.

"Just as the paper reports, sir," stated Mr. Needling firmly. "And may I ask who *you* are?"

"Then where is James Rennick?" growled the man, ignoring Mr. Needling's question entirely.

Mr. Needling challenged the man in kind; he too held his tongue.

"*Where*?!" the man demanded again, slamming his hand against the counter.

"And *you* are?!" reiterated the hotel manager, his small bottom lip puckered in defiance.

"Hey!" yelled Sergeant Wilcox as he entered the hotel.

The bearded man spun toward the doorway.

"*James,*" uttered Elsie.

James rushed through the entryway just behind Sergeant Wilcox, sliding to a stop as he set eyes on the bearded man.

"Dad?!" exclaimed James.

Elsie stuffed her sister's letter into her purse and pushed her way past James and the sergeant.

"Elsie!" called James, stumbling after her into the driveway.

"No, James!" she yelled. James watched her shrinking figure as she hurried down the hill. "I've got to think!" she shouted. "I've got to figure this out!"

Chapter 11
VESTA *AND* DORIS... OH MY

UNLIKE THE TENSION that permeated the hotel, the relaxed atmosphere of the Gull's Café offered a perfect retreat for Elsie. She smiled absently as she accepted her latte from the waitress. Spreading her sister's letters across the small, round table, she arranged them in order of date.

"I've just got to think through what I know," she murmured, taking a careful sip of her coffee. "I must sort through the facts to make sense of the whole picture."

Elsie smoothed out a napkin and scribbled a bullet point with her pen. She wrote her first question:

"Why bring everyone together from so long ago?"

She thumbed the curled edges of the napkin as she silently pondered possible answers. Scribbling another bullet, she murmured aloud, "What if I treated each murder on its own? Even the one from twenty years ago."

She lifted her head and moved her small nose about, inching her glasses further up the bridge of her nose.

"Mr. McCray," she whispered, deep in thought. "Norma Kemper. Reverend Pennington."

She brushed her fingers across her sister's most recent letter.

"Justice. Of course it would make sense that the reverend would cite Scripture," she said, a sad smile forming across her face. "The book of Amos."

She tapped one finger repeatedly against her temple.

"The book of Amos," she repeated. "*Amos.*"

She dropped her head into her hands and laughed.

"*Of course!*"

"How is everything, ma'am?"

Elsie flinched, lifting her eyes.

"Oh, I'm sorry. I didn't mean to startle you," said the waitress.

"No, it's all right," she replied as she swept her hair behind her ear. "I was just lost in thought." Elsie lifted her drink. "The coffee is perfect, thank you."

The café's door chimed to reveal Mrs. Tidwell and Mrs. Malford bursting across the threshold.

"Oh, no," uttered Elsie.

"Ms. Maitland!" Mrs. Malford waved, weaving through the tables with Mrs. Tidwell in hobbled hot pursuit. "Lisette, two cups of tea, please."

The waitress nodded as Mrs. Malford slid into the chair opposite Elsie.

"You're not using this?" asked Mrs. Tidwell, borrowing a chair from the neighboring table. "Oh, Ms. Maitland! It's so nice to see you!"

"And a basket of muffins, please," called Mrs. Malford, waving at Lisette.

Mrs. Tidwell leaned forward, resting her hand upon Elsie's.

"Are you quite recovered?" she asked. "From your horrific—*horrific* ordeal?"

"Yes, *indeed*," said Mrs. Malford. "I *heard*." She tilted her head forward and peered furtively over the rim of her glasses. "How is your arm?" she whispered.

"It's better," replied Elsie slowly, sliding her hand out from under Mrs. Tidwell's. "In fact I was just trying to take some time away..."

Mrs. Tidwell leaned in more closely.

"...away, with a bit of time to myself," hinted Elsie further.

"I agree, Ms. Maitland," said Mrs. Tidwell, squeezing her shoulder. "And you *should*."

"All that you've been through," agreed Mrs. Malford, happily accepting the basket of muffins from Lisette, who glanced regretfully in Elsie's direction.

"I still can't believe it," said Mrs. Malford. "Iradene Hartwell." The florist broke off a piece of a muffin between her fingertips. "My *my*."

"Tell me," said Mrs. Tidwell, sliding forward in her chair, "how did you know? To look in Paul Hulling's room, I mean? Was he... Did he seem..." Mrs. Tidwell's eyes narrowed, "...*suspicious* to you?"

"Oh, *thank you*, Lisette," said Mrs. Malford, inhaling the aroma of her tea.

Elsie discreetly slid her sister's letters into a neat pile and turned them over. "No," she replied to Mrs. Tidwell's question. "I just had a hunch, I suppose. I didn't necessarily suspect Mr. Hulling of anything at the time."

With cheeks bulging from a mouth full of muffin and being so excited to contribute to the conversation, Mrs.

Malford blurted her question: "Roo do row that Rarian is recowering?"

Elsie's eyes widened. "Excuse me?"

"Doris was wondering if you already knew that Marian is recovering," translated Mrs. Tidwell. Mrs. Malford nodded, pointing her finger toward Mrs. Tidwell appreciatively. Mrs. Tidwell continued: "It was arsenic that poisoned that poor dear; small amounts over a long period of time—just like with poor Norma."

"A different poison?" asked Elsie. "The doctor told you?"

"Oh no, it was written up in the *Tribune*." Mrs. Tidwell retrieved the paper from her purse. "You see why it's so critical we have access to all possible sources of information?"

"Thank goodness, *indeed*," confirmed Mrs. Malford articulately, her mouth now free of muffins. "If my husband hadn't taken the train into town this morning we wouldn't have had a paper at all!"

"Somehow I doubt that," replied Elsie.

Mrs. Tidwell went on. "They say Iradene Hartwell won't speak without her lawyer, but they strongly suspect that she was poisoning that poor girl."

"Which one?" asked Mrs. Malford.

"Marian, of course!" exclaimed Mrs. Tidwell. "Who else?"

"Norma."

Mrs. Tidwell was taken aback. "Yes, that's true." She paused thoughtfully for a moment. "Why *did* she murder Norma?"

"That is a good question," said Elsie.

"Because of what she knew," said Mrs. Malford, pouring her tea.

Elsie and Mrs. Tidwell turned rapt attention toward the florist.

"Walton," said Mrs. Malford. "Walton, the chef at the hotel, said that Norma was bragging about coming into money just before she was murdered."

Mrs. Tidwell gasped. Mrs. Malford's eyes grew wide and she stretched her neck across the table like an old turtle who has been dealt a great shock.

"Oh *really*, Vesta!" she exclaimed in disapproval. "What *have* you been doing?"

"Being laid up in bed is what I've been doing! Going stir-crazy in that house of mine!"

"What did she know?" asked Elsie, rerouting the conversation.

Mrs. Malford shook her head. "No one knows," she replied.

"Could have been anything with that nosy girl," murmured Mrs. Tidwell, taking a sip of her tea.

Elsie turned her eyes on Mrs. Tidwell.

"Oh… I meant to say that *poor* girl," Mrs. Tidwell corrected. "Bless her soul, that sweet, young thing. Saved me when I had my accident, you know? Fell from a tree. Did I tell you? I live on Shady Glen Road, not far from here, and I was trimming my apple tree—"

"Mrs. Malford told me," interjected Elsie hastily.

Mrs. Tidwell reflected. Then she remarked sadly, "I never did hear what Mr. Humphreys and his *mistress* were arguing about. Just bits and pieces. I think he wanted to end things? Too risky, the wife finding out, but I'd be shocked to learn that the wife didn't already know! I mean it's fairly common knowledge now—Mr. Humphreys coming by to 'fix' her leaky faucet." Mrs. Tidwell scoffed. "I've never heard of a woman having that much faulty plumbing in all my life."

Mrs. Malford rapped her fingers against the tabletop. Hurriedly she gulped down a mouthful of tea.

"You haven't heard!" she exclaimed, gasping.

"Heard what?" demanded Mrs. Tidwell.

Mrs. Malford swept a napkin across her lips. "Mr. Humphreys couldn't have been the one arguing with Ms. Sanders!"

"What do you mean, Doris!?"

Elsie sat quietly, her eyes shifting back and forth between the two ladies.

"Mr. Humphreys was *out of town*. It must have been someone else meeting with Ms. Sanders!"

"You don't say!" exclaimed Mrs. Tidwell.

"But I just did," said Mrs. Malford, puzzled.

"Then *who*?" questioned Mrs. Tidwell.

"Enough about all that for a moment," said Mrs. Malford. "You know there are other happenings around town besides those murders at the hotel, right? Did you hear about Mildred?"

"I did! I can't believe she would have done such a thing!"

Elsie stood; it was clear that Mrs. Tidwell and Mrs. Malford had all new gossip to discuss. Mrs. Tidwell turned her head, startled to be reminded that there was a third party at 'their' table.

"It was a pleasure seeing you both," remarked Elsie, replacing her letters in her purse. "I think I will just take a walk. The weather really is beautiful outside."

"Of *course*, dear," said Mrs. Tidwell. "And you let us know if you need anything. Such a *horrific* ordeal you went through."

"You poor girl," agreed Mrs. Malford, nodding as Elsie slung her purse across her shoulder.

Before Elsie could fully depart, Mrs. Tidwell turned back to her friend and eagerly resumed their conversation.

Mrs. Malford stated firmly, "There's no smoke without fire, you know."

Elsie stilled.

"Mrs. Malford," she said.

Mrs. Malford peered over her shoulder. "Yes, dear?"

"What did you just say?"

"What? That there is no smoke without fire?"

"That's it!" exclaimed Elsie.

At the mention of this phrase, everything concerning the murders suddenly connected in Elsie's mind.

"There's no smoke without fire," she murmured excitedly, pressing the palm of her hand against her forehead. "There is no smoke without fire, *unless* it's a smokescreen!"

Chapter 12
THE GUESTS RECONVENE

CONFIDENT WITH HER newfound information, it did not take Elsie long to convince the initially reluctant Sergeant Wilcox to reconvene the guests in the hotel dining room. The mood was at best unsettled as each awaiting guest grew more suspicious as to the reason for this meeting.

"I hope you've got something solid, Ms. Maitland." Sergeant Wilcox said, tugging irritably at his belt. "As far as I'm concerned we've apprehended our killer."

"I understand," replied Elsie. "And I think you have caught *one* of the murderers, sir."

The sergeant was doubtful but took a seat at the dining table beside Ms. Maitland.

"That's everyone," announced Mr. Needling, drawing the dining room doors closed. He swept an unsteady hand through his hair. "Shall we begin?" he asked, taking a seat.

Elsie studied the guests briefly before standing.

"Thank you all for being here," she began. "I know that

this is not customary in circumstances such as this, but I can assure you that the information I've learned is significant."

Mr. Turnbull shifted in his chair.

"And why, exactly, did this information require our presence?" he interjected. "Certainly you could have passed this information on to the sergeant. He's a capable man; he can do with it what he pleases."

Sergeant Wilcox glanced approvingly.

"Yes, that's true," agreed Elsie, turning toward the sergeant. "But, you see, what I've learned affects almost everyone here, and it's something—"

"Wait! Wait!" came a voice from outside the dining room doors.

Mr. Needling rose from his seat as the dining room doors slowly opened. Mrs. Tidwell was hunched over in the doorway, her hands pressed against her knees as she gasped for breath.

"Mrs. Tidwell!" exclaimed Mr. Needling. "This is a *private* meeting. I am going to have to ask you to leave this instant!"

"That's Vesta Tidwell," whispered James to the man beside him. "One of the town gossips."

The man nodded, stroking his beard.

Mr. Tidwell bustled into the room with perspiration settled on his forehead.

"I'm *so* sorry about this," he said between labored breaths. "I only just realized my wife had come up here, but I tried to stop her."

"Why can't we just *leave?*" grumbled Olivia Welling to her husband.

"We've come this far," he replied. "Might as well see it through."

"All right, Mrs. Tidwell. Let's go," said the sergeant, standing.

"Oh! But—" Mrs. Tidwell's expression fell. "But I've come all this way. I've practically *run*—"

"Completely against doctor's orders!" exclaimed Dr. Linder.

Paul Hulling looked on in astonishment.

"Sergeant, could we just have them stay?" asked Elsie.

The sergeant glared at her and said through clenched teeth, "I don't think you understand what you're asking, Ms. Maitland."

"I'm aware," she replied. "*But* Mrs. Tidwell has actually been a great help in uncovering the truth."

"Thank you, my dear!" exclaimed Mrs. Tidwell. "Come, George."

Mr. Needling sank into his chair.

"Ms. Maitland, you better know what you're doing," murmured the sergeant.

From the head of the table, Elsie turned to face the rest of the guests.

"I think almost everyone here would like to know *why* the same guests from a twenty-year-old murder case were reunited at the very hotel in which the murder took place."

"And *you* know?" asked Sergeant Wilcox doubtfully.

"I do. You see, it's the way I think," she explained. "It comes naturally to me to piece seemingly meaningless scraps of information together much like a puzzle. It's…" Elsie paused. "Really, it's more like I think in webs. Once I've learned something, things just *connect*."

"Tell us what you found out," encouraged James.

Elsie retrieved her sister's letters and spread them across the table.

"With the help of my sister I have been able to consider this case from various angles. It was something Reverend Pennington said that actually broke this case wide open. The reverend quoted a verse of Scripture before he was murdered, a verse from the book of *Amos*."

"Mr. Needling," she began.

His small eyes darted swiftly toward Elsie.

"What is the name of your gardener?"

"Amos Hartin." A perplexed look swept over his face. "Why? Has he got something to do with this?"

"Unknowingly, yes," replied Elsie.

She retrieved a small medicine bottle from her purse.

"When I first arrived at the Hotel Westend I made a visit to the pharmacy. It was by sheer happenstance that I overhead your gardener, Mr. Amos Hartin, discussing the contents of a medicine bottle he had found in one of the hotel's flower beds."

"In the *flower beds*?" questioned Mr. Needling.

"In the flower beds," confirmed Elsie. "I too thought this was strange."

"It certainly is!" he exclaimed.

"The pharmacist assured Amos, however, that his discovery wasn't something to be especially alarmed about, as it was a fairly common medicine often used to help someone sleep."

"But why was it buried in his flower bed?" asked Olivia Welling.

"*Exactly*," said Elsie. "And that's how Amos, unintentionally, got the ball rolling."

The guests looked curiously at each other. Elsie continued:

"We need to treat each murder as an individual case. First, let's consider Reverend Pennington, and let's consider the 'how'. Reverend Pennington was killed by a blow to his head. As terrible as it is, the cause of death is quite straightforward. Now, let's consider the maid, Norma Kemper. Mrs. Tidwell informed me that she died from ingesting the poisonous herb, white snakeroot. Is that correct, Dr. Linder?"

Dr. Linder shifted uncomfortably in his chair.

"That's right," he confirmed. "Ms. Kemper received doses in small increments until she died. In fact, white snakeroot is easy enough to obtain as it comes from a natural plant source. Anyone could conduct basic research to verify its toxicity just as easily as one could research the hazards of poison ivy, for instance."

"And I'm sure", added Elsie, turning to Sergeant Wilcox, "upon receiving this information you determined the method in which this poison was administered to Norma."

"Of course," replied the sergeant. "The hotel's chef, Walton, mentioned that Norma was in the habit of taking sleeping pills before bed, so naturally we checked to make sure her pills were as prescribed. Although her prescribed bottle did indicate sleeping pills, the labs proved that the contents of the bottle were in fact capsules filled with small doses of white snakeroot."

"Then what of Ms. Marian Hartwell's poisoning?" inquired Mr. Turnbull.

Paul lifted his eyes.

"She was poisoned by a more commonly known drug," replied Elsie.

"Arsenic," chimed Mrs. Tidwell.

Paul glared at Mrs. Tidwell as Elsie went on.

"It has already been determined that Marian Hartwell was being poisoned by her own sister, Iradene. In fact, I suspect she was being poisoned long before she even arrived at the hotel."

"That's true," said Paul. "The doctors have determined that Iradene has been administering doses of arsenic into her food for some time now. Only recently has she increased the doses, as Marian's birthday is approaching."

"I could tell the woman was a nut job," said Olivia. "But *why* would she want to kill her sister?"

"Money," stated Sergeant Wilcox. "Iradene and Marian's father left millions to both of them. Iradene, however, was named legal trustee of Marian's portion of her inheritance until Marian became of age or married—whichever came first. Since Marian was getting older Iradene expedited her plan to kill her sister."

"She kept Marian dependent on her, mentally and financially," explained Paul. "So, I hired a private investigator back in New York, to find out what he could on Iradene. He is the one who discovered the will."

"Jonathan Davis?" asked Elsie.

"That's right," replied Paul. "But how did—?"

"I saw his name on the envelope that contained the documents proving Marian's inheritance."

"Then you see why I had to come out here," said Paul. "I knew I needed to show Marian exactly what I had uncovered, and then perhaps she would be willing to sever ties with that woman. Davis called me after having secretly met with Marian at her house, in the gardens. He found out their plans to come here, and he booked the same arrangements for me through Skylark Travel Agency. He also suspected that things were getting worse and that if I didn't get her away now…" Paul pinched the bridge of his nose.

"You got to her in time," said Elsie softly.

Paul shook his head.

"Barely," he murmured. "I just ended up trying to drink away my fears. I thought, what if she still won't come with me? But then when I saw that she was getting sick I secretly called the doctor, making sure Iradene didn't know, of course."

Dr. Linder added: "Ms. Marian Hartwell agreed to see me only after her sister had gone to bed. I had my suspicions that something wasn't right from my first meeting, and they were obviously confirmed when the lab results arrived. That's also why I was on the premises when Reverend Pennington and Norma Kemper were murdered."

Mr. Turnbull stroked his chin. "Yes, that's right," he started slowly. "Now that I think of it, I don't recall seeing Marian at all while we were searching for the child. Yes, I see now. You, Dr. Linder, remained in the room with her."

"That's right," he confirmed. "That is, of course, until I realized I was needed elsewhere, but it was too late to help the reverend and Norma."

"But I still don't understand. Why bring all these people together?" asked James. "Why bring together the same guests from twenty years ago?"

"Yes, and why reenact that terrible murder?" asked Mr. Turnbull. "One can't deny the similarities!"

"Well, it was actually something that Mrs. Tidwell and Mrs. Malford said that gave me the answers to those very questions," said Elsie.

Mrs. Tidwell's eyes widened in excitement. Sergeant Wilcox's expression, however, was doubtful.

"The two women simply mentioned the well-known phrase, 'There is no smoke without fire', *meaning*", elaborated Elsie, "if unpleasant things are said about someone there is probably a reason for it. 'Smoke' can't start from nothing. Rumors can't start unless there is some truth *somewhere*."

"What's your point?" asked Mr. Welling.

"My point is that if someone can arrange for a twenty-year-old *unsolved* murder case to come to life again in a small, gossiping town, people will focus their attention on where *that* fire began. People will focus on the guests from twenty years ago and the victim's family, and wonder where they are now. And wonder who *did* kill Mr. McCray?

"One won't think of Norma's death, for instance, in the simplest terms: the murder of a maid in a small town. One naturally wouldn't think that way because Norma's death *seems* to be tied into an unsolved case from twenty years ago! All the letters received enticing people back to the hotel, all the travel arrangements that were made, the sensational reenactment of the night Mr. McCray was murdered—it was all a *smokescreen* to distract us from the murder with the hidden motive. Norma Kemper's murder."

"You're saying Norma's death had nothing to do with— with this whole reunion?" asked Mr. Turnbull.

"That's *exactly* what I'm saying," confirmed Elsie. "What better way to conceal the true motive of a murder than to muddle it in with a twenty-year-old case that was never solved? The more you try to connect Norma's death to the twenty-year-old murder, the better it is for our murderer! Newspapers would splash wild theories in the headlines and nobody would go back to the basics and treat Norma's murder as a sad, yet deceptively simple, crime. Nobody focused on Norma as just

Norma, a small-town maid who was killed by someone *in* her small town."

"All right," remarked Sergeant Wilcox. "Let's get rid of the smoke. We know that Norma was killed because someone tampered with her medicine. We also know that she was suddenly coming into an unexplained source of money in the near future."

"Blackmail?" suggested Paul.

"That would be my guess," agreed Mr. Welling.

"That means she knew something about someone," said Elsie. "So now I have to ask myself about the murderer and the *smaller* details he arranged. We need to separate the smoke-screen of the twenty-year-old case from the deliberate planning needed to kill Norma."

"Just a moment," interjected Mr. Welling. "I see what you're saying, and the concept makes sense, but isn't all this just speculation? I mean, for your theory to be correct, you would first have to know for *sure* that a local person was actually behind all this."

"I agree," replied Elsie. "In fact, the tape recorder that was used to play the sound of a baby crying was my proof that a local person was behind the murder."

"The tape recorder?" asked James, surprised. "I know that Mr. Needling was paid to collect the tape recorder from a phone booth in town, but how does that actually prove that the murderer is from here?"

"*You* started that tape recorder?!" yelled Mr. Welling, sneering at Mr. Needling.

"Wait! Let's not get into that right now," interjected Sergeant Wilcox, lifting his hands. "Let's stay focused."

Mr. Welling kept his eyes on Mr. Needling.

Elsie continued: "What was significant to Norma's murder was that the murderer arranged for Mr. Needling to collect the tape recorder from the phone booth on Shady Glen Road. Why there? He could have just mailed the package to the hotel."

"He probably didn't want the authorities to trace the package if he mailed it, and he certainly wouldn't want to drop it off", suggested Paul, "for fear he might be seen."

"Valid point," agreed Elsie. "But if a murderer is trying to draw attention away from himself and the true motive for his crime, my guess is that he would need to cast suspicion on someone else."

"So", said James, "you're saying the murderer essentially *sent* Mr. Needling to collect the package in hopes that someone would see him with something in his hands on the night of the murder? So Mr. Needling would serve as prime suspect?"

"Not *hoped*," said Elsie. "I believe our murderer *planned* on it. Mrs. Tidwell mentioned that she lives on Shady Glen Road and, it occurred to me, who better to make note of a man walking in the middle of the night with a package in his hand than Westend Bay's very own bloodhound?"

Sergeant Wilcox chuckled. "It was Mrs. Tidwell who alerted me to Mr. Needling's whereabouts."

"So now we know for sure", said Elsie, "that we've got a local murderer."

"Because no one outside the town would know such specifics about Mrs. Tidwell," murmured Mr. Turnbull.

"All right, Ms. Maitland," started the sergeant. "We know we've got a local murderer. Now let's forget about the twenty-year-old case, and let's talk about who killed Norma."

Chapter 13
NORMA KEMPER'S MURDER

HAVING ALREADY DISCUSSED *how* Norma was poisoned, the guests sat eagerly around the dining table to discover who murdered Norma and why.

Elsie took everyone back to the odd circumstances surrounding Amos's discovery of the pill bottle in the garden.

Mr. Needling threw up his arms. "I still don't see what Amos has to do—"

"Shhh," hissed Mrs. Tidwell. "Let her finish."

"When I saw Amos in the pharmacy he was *following up* with the pharmacist to determine what was in the bottle."

"So?" asked Mr. Turnbull. "Is that relevant?"

"It's extremely relevant, Mr. Turnbull, because I—and the majority of the guests—had *only just arrived* at the hotel by that time. Therefore, Amos must have found the sleeping pills and given them to Mr. Reddy, the pharmacist, for analysis sometime *before* many of us arrived to the hotel."

"I still don't see..." started Mr. Needling, frowning.

"Remember, Norma's sleeping pills had been swapped out with capsules filled with poison," explained Elsie. "Therefore, the sleeping pills Amos found must have actually been Norma's prescribed medicine. That means our murderer was at the hotel before the guests even arrived. He switched Norma's medicine with poison and immediately buried her actual sleeping pills so as not to incriminate himself. Norma takes what she thinks are her sleeping pills every night, and with each dose she feels worse. On the third night—the night our murderer anticipates the poison will take full effect—he leaves a message for Mr. Needling to collect and play the recording of the crying baby. The maid can't wake up, just like twenty years ago, and, as an unexpected bonus for our murderer, the reverend is killed as well. The smokescreen is set and we start to ask the wrong questions."

"And because of the nature of the poison", said Paul thoughtfully, "the murderer didn't have to show up at the hotel again until *after* Norma died."

"It's a perfect alibi," murmured Mr. Turnbull.

"But *who* is the murderer, Ms. Maitland?" asked Sergeant Wilcox.

Elsie sighed.

"I'm afraid," she said gently. "It's Mr. George Tidwell."

Mr. Tidwell's jaw plummeted toward the floor.

"My—my *dear*," he stammered. "I'm fond of you, but I'm afraid you are very much *mistaken*. Actually, I've never been so insulted," he growled, his gaze fixated on Elsie.

"That's crazy!" blurted Mrs. Tidwell. She turned to her husband. "Ignore her honey, she has no idea what she's talking about."

"Mr. Tidwell", explained Elsie, facing the group, "makes

weekly visits to the hotel to deliver fish. Is that correct, Mr. Needling?"

"Why yes, of course, but—"

"Therefore," continued Elsie, "Mr. Tidwell came to the hotel sometime during the week before all of the guests arrived. It would have been easy enough for him to walk around the hotel unobserved, as he is a frequent visitor in his professional capacity. He delivers the fish as usual, but also finds an opportunity to swap Norma's medicine for the poison. Remember, whenever Mr. Needling is expecting a lot of guests it is usual practice for Norma to both work and stay overnight at the hotel, in her assigned room. It takes but a few moments for Mr. Tidwell to bury Norma's actual sleeping pills in the flower bed and head home. Really, if you think about it, Norma has already been murdered. It's only a matter of waiting for her to take a few of the capsules and mask the crime with the sensation of the twenty-year-old case."

"This is absolute *nonsense*," hissed Mr. Tidwell, now standing. "And tell me, Ms. Maitland, what possible motive could I have to kill Norma? Go on, tell me that."

Elsie took a solid step toward him. "Ms. Sanders," she replied coolly.

Mr. Tidwell fell back into his chair as though he had been punched in his chest.

"Ms. *Sanders?*" exclaimed Mrs. Tidwell. "What about Ms. Sanders?!"

"Mrs. Tidwell," started Elsie slowly. "Your injuries were as a result of falling from your apple tree, right?"

"That's correct."

"And it was your maid, Norma Kemper, who returned unexpectedly to the house to retrieve her watch. She discovered that you were injured and, of course, came to your aid. Unfortunately, because of your accident you never had a chance to learn what Mr. Humphreys and his mistress were arguing about in the adjacent house. Norma, however, learned something far greater, and that's when she realized she could make a quick buck."

"I—I don't quite understand," stammered Mrs. Tidwell. "Why would Norma make money from helping me?"

"Not from helping you, Mrs. Tidwell—from what she *saw*."

Elsie explained: "While visiting the local florist shop I met Mrs. Doris Malford, and I learned *quite a bit* about the people of this community! More specifically I learned about Mr. Tidwell and that the community did not believe that he could possibly be happy in his marriage. That's why I even considered Ms. Sanders in the first place."

"I still don't understand..." murmured Mrs. Tidwell, her voice shaky.

"Just think about what we discussed today, Mrs. Tidwell," replied Elsie softly. "Your friend, Mrs. Doris Malford, informed you that Mr. Humphreys was actually out of town the day you fell from the tree, and you asked yourself, 'who then was arguing with Ms. Sanders in her upstairs bedroom?'"

"I considered what Mrs. Malford told me about the day you had your accident. She admired the fact that Mr. Tidwell met you at the hospital just as doctors were wheeling you into the ICU—in other words, *right* after you had your accident. But if Mr. Tidwell was out making deliveries, how *could* he have known about your accident so soon?"

"There was a message for me at my market!" yelled Mr. Tidwell.

"But that's just *it*, Mr. Tidwell," countered Elsie. "You

never made it back to the market. Everyone said you must have gone straight from your delivery route to the hospital, arriving just as your wife was admitted. So *how* could you have known? There was no way the news could have travelled *that* fast, even in such a small town. The *only* way you could have known about your wife's accident immediately after it happened was if you *saw* it happen—if you were *there*."

Stirring in his seat, Mr. Tidwell's chest rose and fell, his face seemingly flushed. But he said nothing.

"And that's when I realized," added Elsie, turning toward the other guests. "Suppose Mr. Tidwell was as unhappy in his marriage as the town proclaimed. Could it be possible that *he* was actually the man upstairs in Ms. Sanders' room? That would explain how he knew so quickly about his wife's accident. Perhaps *he* was the man who was actually having an affair." Elsie turned toward Mrs. Tidwell. "What if the man that you, Mrs. Tidwell, thought was Mr. Humphreys was in fact your own husband?"

"*Not George?!*"

Mrs. Tidwell shook her head adamantly.

"Of course it wasn't me, Vesta!"

For the first time in Mrs. Tidwell's life she was unsure of what to say. Elsie paced as she explained further.

"I believe that Mr. Tidwell was in the upstairs room with Ms. Sanders. Perhaps he might have been trying to end his affair. I don't know, but the reason became irrelevant once Norma caught a glimpse of Mr. Tidwell through that window. I imagine Mr. Tidwell briefly peered outside when he heard the commotion of Mrs. Tidwell falling from the tree—it would be a natural reaction. Unfortunately for Mr. Tidwell, Norma saw him and his secret was suddenly in her hands. Mrs. Tidwell even mentioned that Norma was a 'nosy' individual. She had no qualms about snooping around the houses in which she worked, and she certainly wouldn't let a good piece of information like that go to waste. After all, she made no secret of the fact that she wanted to leave this town. Only Norma and Ms. Sanders knew about the affair, but the difference with Norma was that Mr. Tidwell knew she wouldn't keep quiet about it. He had to silence her."

Elsie turned back toward the group.

"Still, I did have one reservation. If Norma *did* tell Mr. Tidwell's wife about his affair then his marriage could possibly end. I debated on this for some time because, if Mr. Tidwell was having an affair, how much did he really care for his wife in the first place? Did he really care enough about the survival of his marriage to pay blackmail? Enough to *kill* to keep the affair silent? No," Elsie shook her head. "I decided that didn't make any sense. I couldn't imagine that such a motive was strong enough. But then I remembered the Empire Club."

"The Empire Club?" uttered Mr. Turnbull. "Haven't been there for years! But good scotch. Yes, very good scotch," he mumbled quietly to himself.

Olivia rolled her eyes.

"The gentlemen of the Empire Club have a theory, Mr. Tidwell," continued Elsie without pause. "While many women in the town view you as the gentle, long-suffering husband, the men have unanimously decided that you have stayed married for the money."

"Money?" asked the sergeant, straightening.

"The money Mrs. Tidwell is expected to inherit from a distant uncle," explained Elsie.

"That's right," murmured Mr. Turnbull thoughtfully. "I *do*

remember some of the members mentioning that. My, *my*. I just might have to swing by there again sometime."

"*Ah*, so there it is—the *true* motive," expressed Mr. Welling with interest.

Mr. Tidwell made no reply.

"I am expected to inherit a great deal," whispered Mrs. Tidwell, turning to her husband. "Not right away but soon."

"Always has to do with money," murmured Paul disgustedly.

"Is this *true*, George?" demanded Mrs. Tidwell.

"Vesta, I can explain…"

Mrs. Tidwell turned away and faced Elsie once more. Elsie hesitated and Sergeant Wilcox stood.

"I think I ought to have a talk with Ms. Sanders," decided the sergeant.

Mr. Tidwell's eyes remained focused on the floor.

"Don't bother talking to Ms. Sanders," he muttered, rubbing gingerly at the back of his neck. "It's true."

"It's all true, sir?" the sergeant asked.

Mr. Tidwell nodded. Then, standing, he turned to his wife. "I'm sorry, Vesta."

Chapter 14
THE MCCRAY MURDER

ELSIE MAITLAND CLOSED her eyes and sank into one of the dining chairs, listening to the steady rhythm of footsteps as the room emptied behind her.

"Ms. Maitland."

Startled, she opened her eyes to find the bearded man and James standing before her.

"Mr. Rennick," greeted Elsie, standing. She nodded toward Mr. Turnbull who was still sitting in his chair at the table.

"This is my father, Elsie," said James. "I didn't get a chance to introduce you when you rushed out of the hotel earlier."

Elsie was somewhat embarrassed. "Sorry about that," she said with a faint smile. "I had to work everything out, sort through all my thoughts."

"And I see that it worked," replied Mr. Rennick, impressed. "I heard this case was quite similar to the one twenty years ago."

"That's right," confirmed Elsie. "The household was roused

by a baby crying outside, near to the cliffs. They couldn't wake the nanny and, soon after, they found the owner of the house, Mr. Edward McCray, dead in his bedroom."

"In this case, though," added James, "the maid wasn't fortunate enough to wake up."

"Clever of Mr. Tidwell," considered Mr. Rennick aloud. "But it's a shame you couldn't solve the twenty-year-old mystery too."

"Couldn't I?" asked Elsie with some amusement.

Mr. Rennick's brows rose an inch. "You know who murdered that McCray fellow?"

"I do."

She nodded toward Mr. Turnbull.

"Mr. *Turnbull?*" James asked, laughing. "You're kidding!"

Mr. Turnbull seemed unconcerned. "I'm afraid all this sleuthing has gone to your head, Ms. Maitland. You're way off the mark this time."

"Go on, Ms. Maitland," challenged Mr. Rennick, stroking his beard slowly. "I think I'd like to hear this."

Mr. Turnbull narrowed his eyes at the man. "Terrible idea," he grumbled. "The *impertinence.*"

"Mr. Turnbull," insisted Elsie as he peered at her through the corner of his eye. "The first night we had dinner at the hotel you remarked on the unique qualities of various types of fish. You mentioned quite a few."

"That's right," he confirmed sharply. "What's that got to do with anything?"

"Well," started Elsie.

"Yes?" demanded Mr. Turnbull impatiently.

"Among the many things you said, you also mentioned the effects poisonous fish could have on a person, and, to be quite frank, it seems you would know how to kill someone with fish."

James looked at his father in disbelief as Mr. Turnbull's face grew pale.

"Which fish was it, Mr. Turnbull?" asked Elsie. "Which fish did you use to poison Mr. McCray?"

Mr. Turnbull's jaw fell. "You really did put it together," he murmured breathlessly. "But did you put it *all* together?"

Elsie nodded. Demoralized, Mr. Turnbull slumped in his chair.

"Pufferfish," he whispered. "That's what I used—pufferfish."

"So, it's really true?" demanded James. "Why in the world would you kill that man?"

"No. No, you're wrong," stammered Mr. Turnbull, his eyes boring into James's.

"Wait, James, there's more," said Elsie.

Peeling his eyes from Mr. Turnbull, James looked at Elsie with his full attention.

"Think about what was strange about that case from twenty years ago," said Elsie. James hesitated, appearing somewhat puzzled. "What was most strange", she explained, "was the fact that Mr. McCray's wife chose *not* to collect the insurance policy after her husband's death. Why on earth would anyone choose to walk away from a large sum of money that's rightfully theirs? What does an insurance company require?"

James's eyes grew wide.

"Proof of death…" he murmured.

"And *that's* when I realized that Edward McCray was still alive," she said decidedly. "By not collecting the money, it would eliminate any risk of insurance companies exposing fraud."

"But—but the poison?" questioned James. "You just said that Mr. Turnbull poisoned the man, and even Dr. Linder declared Mr. McCray dead."

"That's right, but you weren't near us in the dining room when Mr. Turnbull not only explained the dangers of poisonous fish, but also something far more interesting."

James glared at Mr. Turnbull distrustfully.

"The effects of the poison—pufferfish poison as Mr. Turnbull just admitted—can cause slowed heart rate and a drop in body temperature, to the point that someone might *think* the person that was poisoned is actually dead. That was what happened with Mr. McCray. The only reason Mrs. McCray wouldn't have collected the insurance money was if her husband wasn't really dead."

James paced slowly.

"So Mr. Turnbull", he clarified, "*did* poison Mr. McCray, but…"

"…but he didn't actually kill him," finished Mr. Rennick.

"That's right," confirmed Elsie. "Everything—this case and the more recent one—has been about deception, misleading others to believe what they want them to believe."

"Remarkable," murmured Mr. Turnbull quietly. "Clever girl."

"This is all incredible," remarked James. "But can you explain *why?*"

"I expect it had something to do with Iradene Hartwell. Remember, she was also a guest here twenty years ago. The general consensus concerning Ms. Hartwell is that, along with being an unlikeable woman, she is also a blackmailer."

"That's right," confirmed James.

"I suspect that Mr. Edward McCray was being blackmailed

by Iradene. So you, Mr. Turnbull," continued Elsie, turning toward him, "you and Mr. McCray, as close friends, devised a way to get him out of being blackmailed."

Mr. Turnbull closed his eyes, drawing in a steady, slow breath.

"That malicious woman wouldn't have stopped until she bled Edward dry," he murmured, opening his eyes. "The truth of the matter is that Edward was *protecting* his wife from some scandal that would have made her and their family's lives miserable had it gotten out—some political scandal having to do with other members of her family—but she had nothing to do with it. Still, they would have tied her name to it. Obviously I believed her." Mr. Turnbull leaned forward. "He was *protecting* his family by paying the blackmail, but he knew he had to get out of it for good. They all had to get free from that woman so they could live their lives. The only way to do that for sure was to make Iradene Hartwell believe that he was no longer alive to be blackmailed."

James was stunned. "It's unbelievable," he murmured.

"So you *carefully* poisoned Mr. McCray, putting to use your expert knowledge of the fish's toxin," said Elsie, her eyes still on Mr. Turnbull. He nodded. "You gave Mr. McCray the poison and then, as planned, his body temperature drops, his pulse becomes almost nonexistent and he is unable to even move or talk. Dr. Linder quite honestly declares him dead upon examination."

Mr. Turnbull added: "But as for the nanny," he recalled, "she really did make the mistake of taking sleeping pills at the wrong time." He snorted. "The whole scheme was a risk, an *enormous* risk. I couldn't guarantee Edward would survive the poison. All I could do was administer just enough to fool Dr.

Linder—after that, it wasn't in my hands. I tried to divide the doctor's attention at least somewhat as he made his diagnosis. Fortunately, with all the commotion he was noticeably shaken (although I doubt he would admit it). I even insisted on Mr. McCray's heart condition to direct everyone's thoughts to natural causes."

"The power of suggestion," remarked Mr. Rennick.

Mr. Turnbull hung his head. "He could have died," he recalled. "He *easily* could have died, but, as you've discovered, he didn't. We pulled it off all right in the end."

"What did you do?" demanded James. "Just removed the body and *hoped* he would come around?"

"Of course not," answered Mr. Turnbull sharply. "Edward and I had already made arrangements with a doctor. That doctor was standing by to take care of Edward *immediately* after we got there—and we did so as quickly as humanly possible."

"Bribes," interjected James. "By 'arrangements' you mean that you paid them to help you and keep quiet."

"Of *course* we paid them off," hissed Mr. Turnbull. "They were in it as deep as we were, so they were happy to just take the money and keep quiet." He tugged at his shirt collar and started again slowly. "We required one individual to cover for us at the funeral home, the sergeant to drop the investigation, and a doctor—besides Dr. Linder, obviously—to actually care for Mr. McCray as his body fought against the poison. Like I said, it was an *enormous* risk all around, but when Mr. McCray survived the first 24 hours I knew he would probably make a full recovery."

"So then you assisted *Mrs.* McCray in quickly arranging the funeral and, soon after, she and her child moved away," said James.

"That's right. She received quite a large sum of money from Edward's company and they could settle anywhere they liked."

"And there's a bit more," added Elsie grimly.

"*More?*" said Mr. Rennick, his eyes widening.

James dropped back into his seat. "Is that possible?" he murmured.

"As you already know, this place was once known as Westend Manor, but it was sold and converted into a hotel," she explained gently, peering at James. "What I found interesting was that Mr. Turnbull became its *only* live-in resident. It was clear that the owner was generous in making such arrangements for Mr. Turnbull, and *only* for Mr. Turnbull." Elsie turned to face him. "I saw you both... on the cliffs."

"*Who* was on the cliffs?" asked James.

Mr. Turnbull groaned, dropping his face into his hand.

"James," said Elsie, "it was only when I discovered the hotel owner's name that all the small details gradually connected."

"What's this about, El?" he demanded.

Elsie set her eyes on the bearded man.

"The owner of this hotel is your father, Mr. Ted Rennick."

James bounded from his seat.

"That can't be..." he uttered, turning to face his father.

Ted Rennick did not reply.

"Ted", added Elsie softly, "is also a nickname for Edward, as in the first name of Edward McCray—your father."

Chapter 15
CASE CLOSED...NEW BEGINNINGS

THE FOLLOWING MORNING Elsie loaded her luggage into her small, red rental car. Digging for her keys, she smiled as her fingertips grazed her sister's letters. Pulling them from her purse, she beamed as she appreciated the beautiful handwriting.

"Elsie!"

James's shoes crunched across the gravel as he hurried toward her.

"You're not leaving yet, are you?" he asked.

"I am actually. I think I need to go home and take a vacation," she said, smiling. "I was going to tell you I was leaving. I was just loading the car first."

James nodded and stuffed his hands into his pockets.

"But hey," she started, her eyes gleaming, "what about your big story on Olivia Welling?"

James seemed surprised.

"What?" asked Elsie, "You didn't think I wouldn't find out

about that, did you?" She closed the trunk of her car. "After all, I've got connections with Mrs. Tidwell, Mrs. Malford *and* Sergeant Wilcox."

James laughed.

"I can't say I've made as much progress as I had hoped," he admitted.

"Do you know if she was actually married?" asked Elsie.

"No, I don't know for sure, but I decided not to pursue it. I figured sometimes some secrets are better left untold. We've all got secrets…"

"That's a dangerous sentiment coming from a journalist," joked Elsie.

"What can you do?" he said, smiling. "Besides, I've got my own story to work out."

Elsie's cheeks warmed as she caught him studying her.

"Are you going to be all right", she asked, clearing her throat, "with what you've found out?"

"I think I'm still in shock," he admitted. "I'm a little angry, and also a bit bewildered. But it doesn't change the fact that he has always been a good dad." He was silent for a moment and dug his toe into the gravel. "I'll have to wrap my mind around all this, and I've got a ton of questions for my parents. My dad may have faked his own death, fooled a whole town and lived a secret life without my knowing, but hey, what can ya do?"

He gave a lopsided grin.

"Yeah, I'm sorry, James," replied Elsie.

"*Oh,*" he recalled, lifting his eyes. "Apparently, Mr. Turnbull recognized me immediately when I arrived at the hotel. He and my father have always stayed in touch; he's sent him photos over the years. So when Mr. Turnbull saw that I was here with all the other guests from twenty years ago, he called my father. Of course, he came right away… to rescue me."

"I'm sure he knew nothing good could come from this reunion," remarked Elsie.

"And he was right, but there was the matter of Sergeant Wilcox." James grinned. "My dad found that he couldn't do much until someone else was arrested, because Sergeant Wilcox wouldn't have taken too kindly to my dad plucking me from the crime scene and flying me across the country like fugitives."

"Ha! No, I don't think the sergeant would have liked that. You would have been the prime suspect for sure."

A comfortable silence passed between them as James stared absently beyond Elsie toward the cliffs, brushing his fingers across his forehead.

"What are you thinking about?" she asked.

"Mr. Tidwell, actually. Well, sort of." Turning his eyes on Elsie's, he continued, "You know I'm the reason Mr. Tidwell came up with the idea for this whole reunion? He actually recognized me as Edward McCray's son."

"The train station?" she asked.

"The train station," confirmed James.

"It makes sense," considered Elsie. "Mrs. Tidwell did mention that her husband would often bring her a copy of the *Tribune* when he went to 'the station', which would suggest that he travelled by train regularly. And you often take the train just so you can have time to enjoy your crosswords…"

Elsie thought back to her first meeting with Mr. Tidwell and added:

"Mr. Tidwell said that he used to go deep-sea fishing with your dad and Mr. Turnbull, so they spent much time together.

For him, the resemblance between you and your father must have been obvious. At the time, unfortunately, he needed to figure out how to silence Norma, and seeing you sparked the idea to use the McCray murder."

Elsie pondered for a moment.

"But does that mean Mr. Tidwell knew your dad was still alive?" she asked.

James shook his head. "*No*, and he still doesn't know. But I guess that didn't matter for his plan anyway. Simply identifying me as McCray's son was enough. He needed me here because, once the investigation started and they uncovered the fact that I was Mr. McCray's son, their attention would have been entirely on me, at least if blaming Mr. Needling didn't work."

"Just from striking casual conversation with you at the train station," remarked Elsie, "I'm sure it wasn't hard for Mr. Tidwell to learn of your fondness for crosswords. So he lured you here with that fake prize."

"Son returns to seek revenge on all those involved in his father's murder!"

"But can you imagine what Mr. Tidwell thought when he learned that there were in fact *two* murders!" exclaimed Elsie.

James laughed. "*He* probably almost died! I bet he didn't even come to the hotel at his wife's request, he *must have* wanted to know what had happened! This whole thing is amazing, El!" he said, shaking his head. "It's so incredible. *You're* incredible—"

A sudden flush crept across his cheeks. He looked away, his eyes falling on the small stack of letters in Elsie's hands.

"Those are quite a few letters," he remarked hastily.

She frowned, pushing the frames of her glasses further up her nose. "Letters?"

He nodded toward her hands.

"Oh! *Letters*. Yes, with my sister—our letter writing… thing we do." She blushed.

"You know what I think?" said James. "I think I will send Mrs. Olivia Welling a discreet letter, maybe suggesting that she clear up any unfinished business in her past, for her sake and the sake of her marriage. No headlines." James raised his right hand, lifting three fingers proudly. "Scouts honor."

Elsie laughed.

"And *then*," he added, "I think I will write another letter to an *extremely* clever sleuth I know, just to see if she will write back."

"I think you should," replied Elsie. "I've already deduced that she *definitely* will."

<hr />

Elsie found her drive home to be especially subdued after having been through such a heightened experience solving the cases. This lull didn't last long, however, as the familiarity of her hometown brought back the comfort of her daily routine.

As she wheeled her luggage through her front door, she inhaled the familiar scent of her bookstore. Faint yellow lighting washed over the small space, which was illuminated by the few lamps her employee, Lawrence, had left on in anticipation of her arrival. Crossing the hardwood floor, she smiled as the third board near the register creaked in familiar welcome. It was good to be home.

Climbing the winding staircase to the second floor, Elsie entered her quaint, two-bedroom apartment and tossed her keys onto her desk. She headed eagerly toward her bedroom, but stopped suddenly as James's words echoed through her mind.

Be bold… Something you never would have done before.

Elsie rushed back toward her study. Tearing a sheet of paper from a notebook, she scribbled a few words in bold, black ink across the page. Then she hurried back to the door of her apartment, pressed the sheet of paper against its wood, and dialed her phone in excitement.

She stepped back and studied the words, a grin spreading across her lips.

"Elsie!" exclaimed her sister on the other end of the line. "Welcome home!"

"Hey! Listen Franny, I've got an idea…"

Elsie closed the door behind her, the crinkled notebook paper swinging perilously from side to side but holding fast to the small stretch of tape to which it had been hastily attached. It was only as the page gradually settled that its bold words became clear. Resting flush against the door, Elsie's makeshift sign welcomed visitors to:

THE MAITLAND SISTERS DETECTIVE AGENCY

A NOTE FROM THE AUTHOR

Dear Reader,

Thank you for taking the time to read my novel, *The Hotel Westend*.

I understand that your time is valuable, and I truly appreciate that you have chosen to spend it with me and my quirky characters! Furthermore, I hope you will connect with me personally at my website, AshleyLynchHarris.com; I'd love to hear from you.

I have new titles coming your way soon, and with each you'll discover that I love to subtly intertwine my books and short stories. Those who read *The Hotel Westend,* for instance, will catch glimpses of places, events, or characters in my other publications.

Such is the case with my Private Investigator, Hugo Flynn, as he visits Elsie's hometown to solve a case of his own in the *Sherlock Holmes Mystery Magazine* (Stories featuring Hugo Flynn begin March 2016).

Finally, if you did enjoy *The Hotel Westend*, I'd love for you to tell your family and friends about it, and if you have some extra time, I hope you will also post a review on Amazon.

I truly hope you enjoyed getting to know Elsie and her sister, Frances, as much as I have—not to mention all of the suspects…er, I mean other characters in this story. I look forward to connecting with you again soon.

Thank you again for reading.

Ashley

DISCUSSION QUESTIONS

1. Elsie initially began her adventure because of her sister, but now she is in search of her own journey. Can you relate to Elsie? Have you stepped out of your comfort zone and have grown because of it?

2. Reverend Pennington shares a personal story with Elsie regarding justice. In this story he speaks of a vicar and a clever elderly woman he met some time ago. While reading, did you notice that this conversation also served as a tribute to the author's favorite mystery writer, Agatha Christie? [*Murder at the Vicarage*] Where else in Chapter 5 does the author do this? [Hint: *The Body in the Library*]

3. Did you have a favorite character and why?

4. Do you think Elsie should have told others what she uncovered about James?

5. Frances experienced a huge trauma in her life, but over time she has been healing both emotionally and physically. Now she is no longer ashamed of her scars,

but it took some time. Do you agree with the idea that although our experiences shape us, they do not define us? If not, how do you believe our life experiences influence us and our perspectives?

6. Were you surprised by the murderer? Who did you think it would be and why?

BOOK CLUBS

I hope you will consider *The Hotel Westend* for your book club! If so, I'd love to meet with you. Even if you aren't nearby, I would be happy to visit your meeting via Skype or speakerphone.

For more information, please visit www.AshleyLynchHarris.com.

A PERSONAL NOTE

Thanks to *all* my family members and friends who have encouraged me, prayed for me, and celebrated with me.

Thank You, God. *Every* single amazing thing in my life is from You and is Yours.

There have been three people in my life who have wholeheartedly devoted their time, prayer, and energy to not only making this novel possible, but who have also walked with me since the first day I started this writing journey.

To my husband, Alex, your steadfast love and encouragement mean the world to me. Thank you. I love you.

To my parents, Dr. Barrington and Mrs. Janel Lynch, I cannot express how incredibly blessed I am to call you, Mom and Dad. Thank you for the time you have devoted to making this novel possible.

Ashley

ABOUT THE AUTHOR

ASHLEY LYNCH-HARRIS IS an avid reader of mystery fiction, particularly the works of her favorite mystery writer, Agatha Christie. She currently has a series of short stories slated for publication in the *Sherlock Holmes Mystery Magazine*, and *The Hotel Westend* is her debut novel. When she's not writing, Ashley enjoys spending time with family and friends, watching *I Love Lucy*, and studying God's Word. An honors graduate of the University of South Florida, Ashley lives in Tampa with her husband, Alex, and dog, Jo Jo. For more information, please visit www.AshleyLynchHarris.com.

Correspondence for the author should be addressed to:

Ashley Lynch-Harris
P.O. Box 47803
Tampa, Florida 33646

CPSIA information can be obtained
at www.ICGtesting.com
Printed in the USA
LVOW12*1524150816
500453LV00007B/34/P